THE GILDED CAGE

THE GILDED CAGE

LUCINDA GRAY

HENRY HOLT AND COMPANY · NEW YORK

Henry Holt and Company, LLC
Publishers since 1866
175 Fifth Avenue
New York, New York 10010
fiercereads.com

Library of Congress Cataloging-in-Publication Data
Names: Gray, Lucinda (Novelist), author.
Title: The gilded cage / Lucinda Gray.
Description: First edition. | New York : Henry Holt and Company, 2016. | Summary:
"An American farm girl discovers that she's an English heiress but claiming her
fortune leads to danger and intrigue" —Provided by publisher.
Identifiers: LCCN 2015022320 | ISBN 9781627791816 (hardback) | ISBN 9781627791823
(trade paperback) | ISBN 9781627796538 (e-book)
Subjects: | CYAC: Inheritance and succession—Fiction. | Social classes—Fiction. |
Love—Fiction. | Great Britain—History—1800-1837—Fiction. | BISAC: JUVENILE
FICTION / Love & Romance. | JUVENILE FICTION / Historical / Europe.
Classification: LCC PZ7.1.G735 Gi 2016 | DDC [Fic]—dc23
LC record available at http://lccn.loc.gov/2015022320

Our books may be purchased in bulk for promotional, educational, or business use. Please
contact your local bookseller or the Macmillan Corporate and Premium Sales Department at
(800) 221-7945 ext. 5442 or by e-mail at MacmillanSpecialMarkets@macmillan.com.

First Edition—2016 / Designed by April Ward

Printed in the United States of America by
R. R. Donnelley & Sons Company, Harrisonburg, Virginia

1 3 5 7 9 10 8 6 4 2

Special Thanks to Melissa Albert

THE GILDED CAGE

PROLOGUE

I HEFT THE GUN to my shoulder, feeling its familiar weight and the heat of the metal through my dress. Sighting along the barrel, I curl my finger around the trigger. The world shrinks around my target as I breathe in.

Exhaling, I squeeze.

An explosion of sound, and the tin can twenty yards away topples from its perch.

"Told you so, George," I mutter, letting the stock fall to rest on a fence post. The horses in the field alongside me swish their tails, slapping insects from their flanks. The gunshot stilled the relentless cicada hum for a moment; with a hot ticking, it begins again. I reach a hand up to wipe the sweat from my neck.

A shimmering heat haze rises along the rutted track leading from our farm to town, and as I reload the muzzle, squinting at the remaining row of cans, a plume of dust swirls up and takes shape. It's a moment before I recognize the motion as that of an approaching rider.

I smile, making a dash at my hair and dress, slapping the worst of the grime from my skirts. I hadn't thought to see Connor today. But even as I smooth my hair, I realize that it isn't him. The horse is the same shade of chestnut as Connor's mare, but the rider has none of his ease in the saddle.

My stomach turns over. I remember the last time George and I welcomed a stranger to our farm: a doctor who charged too much, who told us nothing could be done. I fight back a rising tide of dread. If George has been hurt . . . But no, if anything's happened, the news wouldn't come from town.

I hold the rifle in both hands, across my body so the rider can see it. He's wearing a jacket and breeches of pale gray, reddened with dust and nicer by far than what my brother wears on Sundays. His hair is pale under his hat, and the beginnings of an unpromising mustache grace his lip. The jacket, store-bought by the look of it, slumps damply about his slight form, and a slender leather case rests over the front of the saddle. If he's armed, I can't see his gun.

As he approaches, he throws up a hand. "Young lady! Hold your fire!" Grinning at me, he reins in the horse with a dusty flourish.

I tip the gun so that its muzzle points to the ground and move toward the steaming horse. "You're far from town," I say to the stranger.

He dismounts, his leather shoes hitting the packed earth with a thump. I'm no longer afraid, just curious—this fellow couldn't best a city girl in a fight, much less a farm girl with a rifle. Bowing slightly, he offers his hand. His nails are perfect, clean crescents.

"Good afternoon, miss. I apologize for arriving with no prior notice, but I wasn't sure how to announce myself ahead of time." He gestures around, as if to underscore the lack of a postbox. "My name is Herman DeLaney. I'm a solicitor with Cryer and Thompson, and I've come to you from New York City."

He says this with a satisfied air that I'd take more seriously from a larger man.

"I'm Katherine Randolph," I say. "And I come from right here." I hold my dirt- and oil-smeared hand out partway, waiting to see whether he'll take it. After a moment's hesitation, he does.

As I tie his mount to the hitching post, he runs his eyes over our house. I see it as he does: sun-bleached boards, dilapidated but well kept. A sagging porch, though freshly swept. And lovely painted flowers winding up from the house's baseboards—our flower beds haven't thrived in the heat, but my brother's artistic talents produce blooms far lovelier than anything I could have grown.

I call the man's attention back from the flowering boards. "Mr. DeLaney, I must ask. For what purpose have you traveled all the way from New York?"

He turns toward me, a slight smile flickering about his mouth. "Is George Randolph at home?"

"My brother has gone to look at a stallion in Paulstown." I remember that this man is not from these parts, and amend myself. "That's ten miles away. He should be back by evening. You're welcome, of course, to return tomorrow."

The man just smiles and removes his hat, wiping his forehead with a cornflower-blue handkerchief he produces from inside his dusty coat.

"If it's all right with you, Miss Randolph, I believe I'll wait." He sits back on the hitching post with a sigh. "I have something very important to discuss with Mr. Randolph."

"Something so important that it can't wait one day?"

He leans forward, his toes just touching the ground. "Indeed." He taps his leather case with a manicured finger. "Pardon me for being forward, but I believe I am about to change your fortunes."

I feel a confused thrill at his words. What could this beanpole of a city man be carrying that would support his claim? "My brother won't return until well after sundown, sir—and it's far too hot to be left in anticipation."

He laughs at my words, settling himself more comfortably on his post. "Perhaps you're right. You *are* a Randolph, after all. Let's start with this: Have you ever wished to see England?"

CHAPTER 1

"Arms up, dear."

I lift my arms over my head.

"Good," says Cousin Grace. "You'll make no move more sudden than that, and it seems your bosom will stay in place."

I don't see how my bosom has any choice. It and the rest of me are bound fast in a mercilessly tight concoction of cream satin. I keep catching glances of myself in the mirror, and each time the girl I see looks a little less like me. My black curls are pinned up in an elaborate style that leaves my neck bare. I'd almost forgotten the mole in the hollow of my left clavicle. Shimmering white gloves wrap my arms to the elbow, reflecting the glow of the strand of pearls that clings to my throat. Katherine the farm girl is in there somewhere, beneath the finery—I see her in the obstinate jawline, a touch too wide, in the dark gray eyes that can't hide their boredom. Grace surveys my bare arms with satisfaction—though the taut lines of my muscles are still visible, they're slackening from disuse. There are no buckets to heave up from the well here, and someone else chops the firewood.

What would Connor think if he could see me now?

"Arms back down," Grace murmurs as Elsie, our dressing maid, fusses with another hairpin. If I don't turn my head too quickly, her work might just survive the evening ahead.

Grace suddenly shrieks, and Stella scurries out from under her skirts, yapping. "I don't understand, Katherine dear, why you insist on keeping that mutt in your room!"

"Because I love her with all my heart." *And because you can trust animals*, I think but don't say. There's nothing fake about a dog. "Besides, she's very fond of you," I add sweetly.

"Well, the feeling is one-sided. She's got hairs all over my dress."

Elsie flutters over to tend to my cousin's skirts, and I manage a crouch, tickling Stella under her chin. She was a gift from George the day after we arrived in England, and I adore her—she's the only one here even less polished than I am.

I walk to the window and tug aside the thick brocade curtain. The estate sprawls out in the dimming February twilight, a wintry tapestry of browns and faded greens. Over its horizon, to the south, is the quarry that once supplied stone to build the house and many others in the area. It fell into disuse some ten years ago, according to George. At the bottom of the smooth lawns, the lake lies black and still, and the trees beyond carpet the valley in a great swath. The forest of Walthingham, planted two hundred years ago, covers several hundred acres. I hold a hand to the chilly glass, listening to the evening song drifting from the aviary.

There's movement at the forest's edge, something darting from trunk to trunk.

"Someone's in the trees," I say, pointing to the spot.

Grace comes to my side, but when I look again the thing has gone. "I can't see anything," she says.

"I'm sure. . . ."

"Just a deer," she says. "They come sometimes to the lake to drink."

"I think it was a man," I say, staring until my eyes blur and sting, and I have to blink.

In the glass, Grace's reflection flinches. Then two shapes emerge from the trees on the long driveway leading to the house—carriages. "Your guests!" says Grace, her voice light. "We haven't long."

My guests. Cold seeps into my fingertips from the windowpane, and my ghostly, black-eyed reflection stares back at me mockingly. I turn away.

Grace looks me up and down. "Don't furrow your brow. You'll perform just perfectly."

I don't want to perform at all, thank you very much, I think. I'm not a traveling show.

Grace must mistake my strained smile for nerves. "You've done wonderfully over the past four weeks, Katherine. You'll be a sensation!"

Has it been only four weeks since we arrived here? America, and Connor, seem to belong to another lifetime. I feel a swell of guilt, not for being here, but for starting to forget.

"Thank you," I say. "For everything you've done for me."

Grace stands up and adjusts her skirts. She is wearing lace as well, but it is dyed a rich scarlet, and cut higher to her neck. Though she asks me to treat her like a sister, she is technically the same generation as my father—his cousin, in fact. She acts very much like a maiden aunt, steering me patiently through the convoluted channels of English society.

"I have enjoyed every moment," she says. "Now, I must go speak with Mrs. Whiting. Just relax and enjoy the night—we've been over everything that's important. Come along, Elsie."

She sweeps from the room, followed by the serving girl, and I'm alone.

Everything that's important. She means the rules, I suppose, the ones she's spent a month drilling into me. The rules for eating, the rules for dancing, the rules for talking. The way to dress, to curtsy, to be an English "lady" rather than a girl from a farm in Virginia. The rules for snaring a husband, that's what they add up to.

It's a wonder these people can walk in a straight line with so many rules in their heads—but, of course, there are rules for walking, too.

I practice now, stepping toward the mirror, placing one foot in front of the other, trying to maintain perfect alignment from toe to heel. It's harder than it looks, like crossing the slippery log over the creek toward Miller's Pond. All that was at stake back then was a soaking in muddy water.

It's been three months since Herman DeLaney, the lawyer from the city, did indeed change our fortunes. His firm, Cryer and Thompson, took care of all the details—getting us to New York, finding a berth on the *St. Elizabeth*. George and I were simply swept along. I still blush to think of DeLaney's face when I asked how it was all being paid for. "By *you*, of course, Miss Randolph," he'd said with a grin.

I don't think either of us really threw much of a backward glance at Miller's Pond or the life we were leaving behind. Edward and Lila saw us off with tears, and there were vain promises that we would see them again. But after that, we let the current carry us away. During the monthlong wait in New York, I was too busy wandering the streets in awe to think properly about how life was changing. I think the reality began to dawn for both of us during the wretched twenty-eight days we were tossed around on the crossing. The only moment of levity on the whole voyage was when we toasted the New Year with a bottle of wine given to us by Herman. He'd scribbled a note on the label—*May you have a prosperous 1821.*

George had to explain to me five or six times what was in fact quite a simple, if improbable, stroke of luck. A grand-father we hadn't even known had died. Thrown from his horse at the age of seventy, he had died instantly of a broken neck. And with our father, his direct descendant, dead, his fortune passed to us. Now, where we were from, wealth was a relative concept. Just about everyone we mixed with, Connor included, had little, though we all had enough. Maybe the McConnells, with eight horses and twenty acres, were doing a lot better than us. Herman DeLaney, with his handsome town house in Manhattan, was definitely *well off.*

I didn't know what real wealth was, of course.

"What are you doing here, Katherine Randolph?" I whisper.

At the sound of my voice, Stella looks up from beside the hearth, where a fire is stoked hot against the chill. In our old home, we had a single fireplace. This house has more than two dozen. But then, this bedroom is the size of our entire farmhouse. The bedding and walls are done up in dusty gold with warm red accents, and the carpet is a thick plush that I never tire of digging my toes into.

But will it ever feel like a home? I feel like a plant brought in from a greenhouse, potted in strange soil. It's not right, this place, this air. I feel like I'm withering.

A gentle rapping pulls me from my reverie. I turn and see George framed in the doorway, and force a smile. Our elevation to the gentry looks effortless on him, as everything does. He wears a midnight-colored tailcoat, and a collar that drapes his neck in velvet. He used to wear rugged breeches and boots in all weather, but now he's traded them for silk stockings and pointed leather shoes with shining buckles. He is only twenty, four years my senior, but his clothes give him a dignity befitting an older man.

"My grubby George!" I say. "I didn't truly believe the dirt could come all the way off."

He pulls a monstrous face at me. "Look who's talking!"

"It's Grace and Elsie's doing," I say. "Don't come too near or you'll make me a mess again."

"Mother and Father would be so proud," he says simply, and holds out his arm. I know he means well by saying such things, but I wish he wouldn't mention our parents like that. It undermines my defenses, and threatens to make me teary. "Of you also," I reply simply as we clasp arms. My hands look like someone else's—the nails, once kept short by hard work and a hundred little accidents, have grown longer.

"Oh, look," I say, gripping his wrist, where a splotch of cerulean blue is dried onto his skin. "You're letting us down."

"Blast," he says under his breath. "I was doing the vista from the west window."

"I don't see where the blue came in. These English skies seem to be gray most of the time."

He tries to tweak my nose, like he used to when we were small, but I duck out of the way as quick as my styled hair will let me. He knows I'm teasing—George's paintings are something to behold, and at last he's getting the recognition he deserves. Tomorrow we go to London to speak with a curator at the Royal Academy. They've seen the landscapes George painted back home, and already they're talking about exhibiting his work.

In the hallway we meet John, the under-footman, coming from the servants' stairs with an armful of pressed linen. He moves aside and offers a shallow bow as we pass; for a moment, before I lower my gaze, his eyes catch on mine. I find it hard, sometimes, to meet his looks. His sun-paled hair is so like Connor's, and from the back, with their broad shoulders and height, they could be mistaken for each other. But John does not share Connor's easy smile. He often looks sad, I think, when he doesn't know he's being watched.

John's was the first face I saw on English soil, waiting with my cousins the day we docked in Bristol. He'd carried my ancient blue trunk, weathered almost to whiteness, to the waiting carriage.

Now I feel his eyes on my exposed throat, and I am sure I'm blushing. "My lord, my lady," he murmurs. George nods a response. He's adjusting better than I am, learning to treat the servants, as Grace instructed, like part of the furniture.

George's hand is tight on my arm as we reach the stairs—he's more nervous than he's letting on.

"I may need to use that arm again after tonight," I say.

"I'm sorry," he replies. "It's just—are you actually looking forward to this?"

"This is our introduction to society," I say. "Think of it like branding cattle. A sharp pain, then we belong."

"And then to the slaughterhouse?" says George.

From below come the silvery sounds of the hired strings, and the low swell of voices. "They can't scare us, George," I say.

"Can't they?"

"We may not be as fine," I say. "But we're far richer."

We stifle our laughter as we walk down the stairs, and I try my best not to tangle my feet in my dress. The butler, Carrick, is waiting at the doors to the ballroom. Cousin Henry Campion, Grace's older brother, limps from the drawing room to the bottom of the stairs, smartly dressed in his dragoon's uniform. Until we were identified as Randolphs by Crowne & Crowne, the family's lawyers, he was custodian to Walthingham, and since our arrival he's welcomed us with great kindness. I haven't dared ask about his wound, but Elsie tells me he got it fighting in France, and that he nearly lost the leg to infection.

"The young lord and lady are ready for their audience,

I see," he says. "Katherine, you look beautiful tonight! Mr. Carrick, if you wouldn't mind."

George's grip tightens on my arm again as the butler swings open the doors. His voice rings across the room beyond. "Ladies and gentlemen! Lord George and Lady Katherine Randolph!"

CHAPTER 2

"YOU WERE RAISED on a farm, they say. Was it dreadfully messy?" The woman in yellow lace grimaces.

"There was a fair amount of dirt," I reply.

"But surely you knew all the time that your place was elsewhere. You must have felt it. The blood will out, as they say."

"I was too busy, perhaps, to notice it."

"But it's all very romantic, is it not?"

I think the romance would have worn off for Lady Flint after a single winter on our tiny farmstead, but I laugh politely all the same.

The conversation bubbles on, and I look for George across the expanse of the ballroom. I wonder if he has told the story as many times as I have. Of our parents' deaths five years before, our simple life under the kindness of our guardians,

Edward and Lila, and the lawyer's visit that changed everything.

I've met so many people; their faces and titles are a blur. Several are men from Cousin Henry's regiment; others are local landowners and their wives and children. Everyone seems to know each other, which makes sense: George and I are the strangers here.

"It must have been such a shock," says Lord Flint, "living in some dusty shack one moment, and now this." He throws a meaty hand around to indicate our present surroundings.

It wasn't quite a shack, I almost say, but then I suppose, to these people, it probably would be. Over our heads, candles reflect off glittering chandeliers, and the guests move below in a crush of richly clothed elegance and breeding. The evening is going better than I expected. Though I have made a few slips, none have been, in my cousin's parlance, fatal. True, the cords of Grace's neck tightened when I took a glass of champagne *before* George, but she quickly recovered her composure. From time to time she taps me on the arm, with a murmured "Well done," so perhaps I am learning the way of things slightly more quickly than Stella.

My brother is surrounded, as he has been for the last hour, by a group of young ladies and their mothers. It's been dawning on me slowly, what this evening means for him. Walthingham is his; at a stroke he has become one of the most eligible bachelors in the country. He's on display, like one of his own paintings on the wall, and these finely dressed guests are lining up to assess his worth. George and I are in this together for the moment, but soon enough he will be taken from me as well.

". . . and you've encountered *snakes*, I've heard . . ." Lady Flint is saying.

Grace sidles up alongside us. "Forgive me," she says to my companions, "but I must steal my cousin from you for a moment." She takes me by the arm and leads me away. "Lady Flint is but two generations removed from a fortune-hunting lady's maid," she says out of the side of her mouth. "I think we can do better than that." As she steers me between the other guests, I wonder what she would have to say about me and George, if she could see where *we'd* come from. I decide it's best not to think so much, as we reach a plump older man with a rough and ruddy face, standing beside a young, fair-haired woman.

"Mr. Dowling," says Grace. "May I introduce your hostess?"

I hold out my hand, as Grace has taught me, and Mr. Dowling stoops to kiss it. "What a pleasure it is to meet you," he says.

"Mr. Dowling is our local magistrate," says Grace. "And this is his daughter, Jane."

The blond girl offers a curtsy and a smile, her gray-green eyes snapping with intelligence. Her dress is deep blue satin, with frothing underskirts of ivory lace and scalloped black ribbon below the bodice. I like her at once.

"I trust Miss Campion has been taking good care of you," says Mr. Dowling. "Showing you the ropes, as they say."

"Grace has been extremely patient," I reply. "Life here is very different from what I'm used to."

"She'll soon have you singing and embroidering with

the best of them, I dare say." Mr. Dowling nods with certainty. "I sometimes wonder whether my Jane would have benefited from a bit more guidance. Her singing is quite abominable."

But he's smiling as he speaks, and Jane bats his arm playfully. "Father!"

"Though I should add that she is possessed of other accomplishments," continues her father. "Her harpsichord is tolerable."

Jane raises her eyebrows. "My singing voice I inherited from you, Father." She addresses herself to me. "Though my musicianship is beyond repair, perhaps we can join forces to save my embroidery. All my little flowers turn out looking like mud pies."

"I'm afraid my accomplishments only stretch so far as shooting crows and shoeing horses."

I dare not look at Grace's expression, but Jane is grinning. "Let's us two take a turn about the room," she says.

And before I know it, she's sweeping me away from her father and Grace. I try to match her delicate step as we thread between clusters of guests.

"Do you and your father live nearby?" I ask.

"On the Crescent," she says. "It's in the center of Bath. But come, the night's too short to talk about our houses. It's smaller than yours, suffice to say." She nods discreetly toward a tall, slender brunette wearing a delicate pink gown and a sour expression. "That is Miss Livia Collins, normally a rather humorous girl, but just now she's being jilted by that fellow with the unconvincing mustache." She inclines her chin toward a pompous-looking young man wearing brightly buckled shoes and a spray of sparse hair on his upper lip.

I giggle, and forget for a moment to wonder whether I ought to.

"And that is Thomas Evans," she says, pointing to a stocky, square-jawed man in long black tails. "He's heir to a small fortune but best avoided, as his mother is insufferable."

We make our way about the party, and Jane feeds me tidbits of gossip on the guests. I feel almost as though I'm back in Virginia, elbowing George and laughing at a church supper.

As we circle the party, we pass an open door leading to a small morning room, where Grace occasionally visits with her more intimate friends. By the half-light within, I see a tall man. He looks to be made of two colors only, black and white. A dark suit against a pale collar. Long black hair and almost porcelain skin. He's staring at the wall.

"And what about him?" I ask.

Jane frowns. "I've never seen him before. He looks rather serious, though, don't you think?"

A maid bearing a tray of small pastries passes us, and Jane takes one. "Get one now, or the men will eat them all," she advises.

I do as she says. Just then, Jane's father calls her name. We look across the ballroom, to where he stands next to an earnest-looking young man in an aggressively green jacket. "Good Lord," says Jane. "I believe he has hooked me another suitor. You must find out more about our mystery guest, while I make my father remember why he does not try too hard to throw men in my way. Here, take this."

She hands me her pastry and sets off demurely through the crowd. I return my gaze to the young man. His quiet shape in the dim light has a curious gravity to it as I slip through the doorway behind him. The room is cool and quiet after the din of the ballroom, the dusky pinks and greens of its furnishings glowing flatly golden in the meager candlelight. Moving closer, I see that the man is studying a painting on the wall—one that Grace pointed out to me on my first day here.

It depicts my grandfather, the late Lord Walthingham, as a younger man astride a tan horse. He looks much like my father did, only narrower in the face. It would have been a rather classical portrait, but for one detail: crouching next to the horse is a lean black panther. Its body is almost lost in the background, but its steady yellow eyes gaze straight out from the canvas. While I find it strange enough in daytime, it is more unsettling still at night, touched by candlelight. My slipper squeaks on the floor a little, and the man spins around.

"Sorry!" I say.

For the half second he is silent, I take him in. His black hair curls up along his neck and the strong line of his jaw. A lock of it falls over his brow, and for one mad moment I long to push it back for him. "I'm sorry," he says quickly. "I should not be in here. Excuse me."

He turns to walk away.

"No, please stay," I say. "It is I who should apologize, for intruding upon your private moment."

He flushes with embarrassment. "I was just admiring this painting," he says. "I'm afraid such gatherings"—he nods toward the party—"are not to my taste."

"Nor mine," I say. "I try to keep up with all the names, but

I'm still not sure if one lady's name is Arabella or Annabella, and whether so-and-so is an earl or a viscount or a lord." He looks unsure if I'm joking or not, half-smiling and half-frowning. "I warn you, if you tell me your name, I may forget it."

He shuffles his feet uncomfortably.

"But, please," I add, "do tell me it anyway."

"I am William Simpson, a lawyer for your estate. I've been working to put things in order since your grandfather's death. I am very sorry for your loss."

"Thank you, sir. I regret that I was never able to meet him." I gesture toward the painted panther. "Though I find his choice of pet rather odd, don't you?"

For a moment Mr. Simpson frowns. "My lady, that panther symbolizes loyalty and courage. Your grandfather was an exemplar of both."

My irreverence has offended him. "And the horse?" I ask quietly.

His voice softens. "The horse, I believe, is just a horse."

His face, already rather nice, is much improved by a slightly crooked smile, which vanishes too soon.

"Your grandfather's death was a great tragedy," says Mr. Simpson.

I nod slowly, feeling terribly guilty. In truth, I find it hard to summon feelings for a man I never met, and who, for all I know, never knew of our existence. Everyone has been at pains to say he died without suffering, though I wonder if that is wishful thinking. He wasn't found, Grace says, for half a day. It happened in the woods on the perimeter of the estate, and the loyal animal stayed with him until rescuers came looking.

Thinking about it now, the portrait of the proud horseman takes on a macabre impression.

"I haven't been on a horse since I arrived in England," I say, hoping to move the conversation on. "I love riding, though I'll have to learn the English way of it before I can go very far from home."

"I'm afraid I'm not much of a horseman," says Mr. Simpson. He looks at the floor, then at the painting once more, then the floor again. I realize suddenly that I still hold two canapés in my hands, and extend one lamely toward him.

Mr. Simpson looks confused but takes the glazed tier of golden pastry. When he bites into it, a flaking crumb falls onto his collar.

"May I?" Stepping toward him, I brush the flake gently aside with my gloved hand. He stands perfectly still, his chest rising and falling beneath my touch. The cloth, I notice, is rough, near homespun in quality, and slightly frayed at the seam.

"There," I say. I look up at his face, my eyes lingering longer than they should. His skin is perfectly smooth, but for a tiny scar on his upper lip and the faintest grit of stubble coming in. His eyes, a deep blue, are trained on mine. My gaze falls unconsciously to his lips, expecting him to speak.

"There you are, Katherine, at last!" Grace calls from the doorway. "What *are* you doing, lurking in the . . . Oh! Mr. Simpson."

He steps back sharply, as though I've pushed him.

"We were just admiring my grandfather's portrait," I say quickly. Too quickly, perhaps, because Grace's eyes narrow.

"Well," she says, her lips pursed, "Lieutenant Hastings has

been asking after you. The dancing is about to start, and you have promised him the first."

I nod, though I can't remember which one Lieutenant Hastings is, and I long to stay another moment in this quiet room. Instead I must follow her back to the ballroom, leaving Mr. Simpson behind.

"Good-bye, William," I say.

He bows discreetly. "I hope you enjoy your evening, Lady Walthingham," he says. "It's Arabella, by the way. The name you've forgotten."

"What *is* he talking about?" mutters Grace.

The music has shifted to a higher tempo. The lieutenant turns out to be a tall man with pale eyes and a high forehead, whose fingertips brush my bare arm as he leads me into the row of dancers.

"How are you enjoying your first ball, Lady Randolph?" he asks.

"Very much," I say. "Though you must forgive me if I step on your feet."

"I'll forgive you in advance. You look light as a feather, Lady Randolph." He drops his hand to my waist as the rest of the couples line up.

"Were you in my cousin's regiment, sir?" I ask. "He has spoken very highly of his fellow soldiers."

"I am a military doctor, my lady."

Henry stands alongside us, partnered with Jane Dowling, and he leans toward me. "This is the man who saved my leg, Katherine, after I took a musket ball from the French. If it weren't for him, I wouldn't be fit to partner anybody."

Though the music is unfamiliar, the lieutenant guides me

into it effortlessly. Even Henry, on his lame leg, manages ably enough with Jane. Is it just my imagination, or are they standing slightly closer than the other dancers? Certainly, her cheeks have taken on a high flush.

After a few turns, the lieutenant releases me, and another man in uniform takes my arms. I think we've met before, but I can't remember his name.

"And what do you think of England, Lady Randolph?" he says smoothly.

"I'm sure it will feel like home in time."

The soldier laughs. "I'm sure it will. And your brother? He seems to be enjoying England very much indeed."

I look down the line, to where George is gazing at his partner, a beautiful raven-haired girl.

Before I can respond, we have swapped again, and I'm partnered now with Henry. We spin and turn in time with the others.

"You're a natural!" he says. "I hope you have a hard heart."

"Why?" I ask.

"Because you're going to have to refuse an awful lot of proposals before this season is out."

I'm still wondering how to reply to that when he passes me on to a captain called Wilson. I'm starting to enjoy myself. It's nothing like the dances at home, with toothless Christopher on his flute, but the music is easy to follow, and I see Grace smiling proudly from the edge of the room. Jane and my brother dance together, both laughing aloud.

When it's time for Captain Wilson and me to part, he says, "I hope you will have many balls at Walthingham Hall, Lady Randolph. I'll be sorry if this is our last dance together."

I look along the line to my next partner—and my eyes meet Mr. Simpson's. As I raise my brow in surprise, he looks suddenly flustered. His feet halt, then start again, out of time with the music, then tangle with those of Lieutenant Hastings to his right. He can't stop himself from falling at my feet.

The music plays on for a few bars, but when the dancers come to a halt, it does, too, in a discordant stutter.

"I think we have a tumbler!" bellows Lord Flint. His wife beside him lets out a peal of laughter.

As Mr. Simpson picks himself up, I reach to help him. But he pulls himself away, his eyes blazing blue.

"The lawyer's had a bit too much champagne, I think," says Captain Wilson.

"No, it was my fault," I say. "Forgive my clumsiness, Mr. Simpson; I think it distracted you."

He brushes himself down, unwilling to meet my eyes. "The fault is mine, Lady Randolph. I should not be here at all."

He's gone before I can speak, darting quickly through the main doors. As I watch him go, my mouth lifts into an imitation of a smile for the guests still watching me.

Then the music starts up again, and Mr. Simpson is forgotten.

CHAPTER 3

AFTER THE LAWYER'S sudden departure, I find I have little energy for a ball. Though I do my best to dance, to smile, I'm relieved when, at a signal from the butler, the musicians begin to pack away their instruments. Grace sends servants to wake the sleeping coachmen, women in wilted silks lean drowsily into their husbands, and at last the long night is drawing to a close.

George, rosy with drink, throws an arm around my shoulders. "Nothing like being branded, Kat," he says, kissing me on the cheek. "But the only one with a pain on his backside is that lawyer fellow."

I frown at him, teasingly. "It's a long ride to London tomorrow, and I expect you to stay awake for it."

He gently musses my hair and leaves the ballroom, walking with the deliberate gait men use to disguise tipsiness.

I see Henry nodding farewell to Mr. Dowling, who is deep in conversation with a gentleman I know to be a judge. Henry then bows to Jane, taking her hand. I watch the way his fingers linger, wrapped in hers, and the way Jane lifts her eyes to meet his. Yes, there's something there, for certain. I might be unused to this country, but love looks the same everywhere.

"A safe journey home," he says to her.

A few officers are departing together, and they jostle me lightly as they pass.

"My apologies, my lady," one of them says, turning. "But you can't blame us for our haste. The Beast of Walthingham preys on the wicked, they say, so we must rush straight to our beds."

"The Beast of Walthingham?" I say, my skin prickling at the strange name. For a moment I can see the strange shape in the trees again from my window.

"Gentlemen, please," says Grace from her place by the front door. "I advise you not to add the needless frightening of young women to your list of sins tonight."

The men bow at her as they exit, but I can see the sardonic curl of their smiles.

"What did they mean?" I ask my cousin. "What is the Beast of Walthingham?"

Grace sighs heavily. "It's a lot of nonsense. Your grandfather kept a small menagerie of exotic creatures on the estate, and they were sold off after his passing. Some of the servants like to fancy that an animal or two escaped first. Imagining the woods full of ravening beasts gives a bit of flavor to life, I suppose."

Several ladies waiting to make their good-byes look

discomfited by her words. Henry has joined his sister, and he breaks in. "The only animal Grandfather was unable to sell was our African elephant," he says. "His rampages have been the ruin of our west wing, and we go through an extraordinary number of peanuts."

Grace shoos at her brother dismissively, and a few of the guests laugh. But a middle-aged woman in green satin pauses beside me, her lips pursed. "Your cousin's elephant can't explain what happened at Longbrooke," she says darkly.

I know that Longbrooke is a large farm that links to the eastern edge of the estate, a few miles from the house as the crow flies, but this is the first I've heard of any happenings there.

"Enough of that," says Grace, placing a hand on the woman's shoulder.

The visitor tugs it away. "A dozen head of sheep torn up in the night," she says. "Not even eaten. Just torn up, as if in spite."

The jollity of the conversation has suddenly turned ugly, and the faces around me are ugly, too: red with drink, features cast in shadow.

Then the illusion passes. These people are just tired, this woman overwrought. A young man attempts to pull her away from me, toward the door. "Mother, come. It's too late for silly stories."

"Where I'm from, wild animals are a regular nuisance," I say, with as much brightness as I can muster. "George was always running things off our land, and I've killed several rattlesnakes with a shovel."

The young man's uncomfortable silence is more than

made up for by Jane's unladylike guffaw. She turns it unconvincingly into a yawn and looks over to where her father is still engaged in conversation with the judge. "I'm nearly asleep on my feet. Take the air with me, Katherine? I'd like to see the damage done to the west wing up close."

A signal to a servant to bring my coat, and we pass down the front steps into the cool of the night. The parkland is cast in darkness, shadows on shadows. A small part of me is afraid, but deliciously so, thinking of a wild beast stalking the grounds just beyond the house.

Jane takes my arm in hers as we pick our way across the quiet lawn. The air is fresh and cold, and the stars burn icily overhead. We cross great patches of lamplight thrown down from the windows, interspersed with silvery swaths of moonlight.

"May I ask you something of a personal nature, Katherine?" asks Jane.

With everyone else around me so stuffy, her question rather takes me by surprise. "By all means."

"Your father . . . he grew up here. All his life, he was surrounded by *this*." Her hand sweeps across the house, the grounds, encompassing the whole rich life of Walthingham. "How could he have given it all up to risk a life abroad?"

"I don't think he chose to give it up, exactly," I say slowly. "He just happened to choose the wrong wife. My mother was an innkeeper's daughter—they met by chance when his carriage broke down outside her family's tavern. My grandfather did not approve of the match."

Jane's eyebrows arch. "He must have learned to accept it in time, if all of this is now yours."

"A bit late, though," I say. "I never met him. And I think my father would have liked to know he was forgiven before he . . . before they passed away."

We reach the house's west wing, in midrenovation after the destruction caused not by an elephant but by a felled oak tree, lightning-struck during a summer storm. The rebuilding is nearly complete, but great chunks of pale stone from the estate's abandoned quarry still litter the ground.

Jane lays her little gloved hand on mine and looks up at the looming, unlit structure. "It's rather unsettling," she says. Then her face brightens. "So, did you meet any interesting men tonight, Kat? Any likely husbands for the lady of Walthingham Hall?"

She's teasing me, I know, but her tone is fond and knowing.

"My brother was the one on display tonight, not me," I say. "I'm far too young to think of husbands."

She cocks her head, catching me in her frank gaze. "It would be nice if that were true, but trust me—a girl like you cannot remain unmatched for long."

A girl like me? I have never felt less sure of what kind of girl I am. Not one ready to marry, that's for sure. "I'm still adjusting to my life here; I can't think of husbands just yet." I remember the way she looked at my cousin Henry as they spun on the floor. "And what about you?"

"If my father has anything to say about it, I'll be packed off to the first rich man who will have me," she says ruefully. "He thinks only of providing for my material comfort—neither looks, conversation, nor a tendency toward regular bathing impresses him so much as an estate."

"But," I venture, laughing, "what about the man you danced with tonight?"

"I danced with more than one, Katherine," she says coyly—then dips her head, seeming to catch my meaning. "There isn't much to say. Not a promise, exactly, but something very close to it." Her eyes shine with suppressed happiness, and in that moment, she seems much younger and more vulnerable.

There's a flash of movement just beyond the rocks. The laughter sticks in my throat. Squinting into the shadows, I see the shapes of three men approaching, one of them swinging what looks like a wine bottle from his hand. There's something in their determined stride that I don't like, and I take Jane's arm. "Let's keep walking," I say firmly, as we move swiftly past the darkened west wing. I have the sudden, desperate feeling that we won't be safe until we reach the lit side of the house.

Jane has spotted them, too. "Katherine," she says in a whisper, and her hand tightens on my arm. The men are soldiers in smart uniforms. At five yards' distance they step into the middle of the path.

"We thought you might want company," says the tallest of the three, a man with a ropy neck and hair that looks nearly white in the moonlight. The other two are darker, and watch us with a hunger that's worse than words.

When neither Jane nor I respond, the tall man gives an exaggerated bow. "You both look lovely tonight," he says. "That is the kind of thing you girls like to hear, ain't it?"

"Good evening, gentlemen," I say curtly.

As I try to lead Jane around them, they block our progress. I think about screaming. Someone would surely hear.

"It's colder than expected," I say, in a voice that's steadier than I feel. "We'd like to return to the house."

"Surely you'd prefer to spend an hour in our company." The man jiggles his bottle, which contains something stronger than wine. I can smell it. "We've got something that'll warm you up."

I bridle at his words, and have a very Grace-like thought: Does he not recognize who I am? "Surely you're mistaking us for some other women you've met tonight. My friend and I have no wish to enjoy your company."

"You women like to think you're so different, one from another," says one of the dark-haired soldiers, a stocky man. "But when you get down to what counts, you're all exactly the same."

I hear Jane's intake of breath, and a flash of hot rage overtakes me. "If you've ever met a woman who has endured even a moment of your company by choice, then she's nothing like me. I'd rather spend an hour with my head in a hornet's nest."

In a flash, the shorter man lunges forward and grabs my arm. I slap his face hard, and he looks shocked for a moment before he reaches toward me again, his fingers hooking around my scarf. I lift my knee sharply, driving it into his groin.

Though he moans in pain, he still keeps hold of me. As I struggle I can see Jane from the corner of my eye, frozen in place. The man's smell—tobacco and liquor breath—assaults me as I cringe away.

"Remove your hands at once."

The man's voice, coming from behind us, is honey in my

ears. Struggling against the soldier's grip, I turn and see John, in his footman's uniform but no coat, standing upright and empty-handed.

"Bugger off, boy, and polish some boots," says the short man, letting me go to cradle the place between his legs. I quickly move to Jane's side, rubbing the tender skin of my throat.

John holds his ground, his face shadowed and unreadable. "First I'll escort the ladies back to the front of the house," he says.

I hear the dreadful *snick* of steel as the blond soldier pulls his sword. "Walk away," he says, his voice dripping disdain.

John stands straighter, moving slowly toward us. "I will not," he replies.

Just then, Henry rounds the corner of the house. When he sees us he pauses a moment, his eyes sweeping over our figures in the moonlight and the drawn sword. Then he speeds forward, despite the painful-looking roll of his hip, moving his body in front of Jane's.

"You call yourselves men of the king's army," he spits in a cold fury. "Put up your sword and leave at once, and do not expect to be welcomed at Walthingham again. You'll be lucky if you don't lose your commissions."

The sword wilts in the fair-haired soldier's hand, and his two comrades step back, their heads bowed, but make no move to leave. Henry reaches down and grabs a chunk of rock, lobbing it at their feet as though he were driving off dogs. "Get off this property! Now!"

The men slink back into the shadows of the house. My

heart thumps painfully in my chest, and I can't stop touching my neck.

Jane clutches at Henry's arm, tears standing out in her eyes. "Thank you, sir. They were horrible. I . . . I could hardly breathe. . . ."

Henry steps close to her, shielding her with his arms.

"John, too, should be thanked," I say faintly, my heart still hammering. But when I look around to do so, he has vanished.

Henry murmurs to Jane, too softly for me to hear, as we walk back around the house.

As we move into view of the last few departing carriages, Henry, still supporting Jane, pauses. "Please allow me to speak to your father about this terrible event, Jane. It happened on our grounds, and I want the chance to apologize to him for it."

She nods without speaking, and Henry moves away toward Mr. Dowling.

"It was a horrible ending to a lovely evening," I say.

Jane attempts to smile. "Please don't think me forward, Lady Katherine, but should you want company, or find yourself in town, you must come and visit me. We girls should stick together."

"That would be lovely," I say.

She takes my hand, pressing it tightly between hers. "I mean it," she says, her eyes serious.

I smile back. Her offer seems heartfelt, and I wonder if it has something to do with the ordeal we have just endured together, or the bond she appears to share with my cousin Henry. In whatever case, I feel grateful to have made a friend this evening with whom I can speak freely. She is as unlike Grace as chalk is to cheese. "Will you be here for the shoot?" I ask her. "It's in a few days' time."

Jane's wry smile returns. "It's hardly a pursuit I relish—blasting defenseless creatures from the sky for sport—but I can accompany my father if you wish."

I draw my hand from hers. "Yes, you must," I say.

"Coming, Jane?" calls her father.

"Yes, Papa," she says, before leaning closer to me. "The dear old thing loves a good shoot. Luckily, so do the birds, when he's brandishing his gun. I doubt he could hit a chicken at five paces."

Laughing, I wish her good night, and she heads for her carriage.

While the horses take her away, I walk into the house and straight up the main staircase.

My room, lit by a crackling fire, is stifling after the crisp outdoors. Elsie dozes by the hearth, a book sprawled open across her chest. When I enter, she stands, yawning.

"Oh, Lady Katherine," she says sleepily, tucking the book away. "Was the ball as lovely as you hoped?"

I struggle to think back to the warmly lit dance floor, the smiles of the crowd. A girl's first ball ought to be remembered as a remarkable thing—and it was an experience Elsie could never share. I force a smile for her benefit. "It was beautiful. I'll tell you about the dresses tomorrow."

"You look very pretty," she says wistfully. "I like your hair like that, all falling loose."

Impulsively I reach for my fan, which rests on the dressing table. "Please, take this."

Her face falls. "Pardon, my lady?"

I continue to hold it toward her. "It's a gift, to show my gratitude. For everything you've done, everything you've helped me with since I got here."

She shakes her head and backs away, as if she's actually frightened of the fan. "I couldn't, my lady. It wouldn't be right."

"Nonsense," I say. "Please, take it."

After a moment her reluctance blooms into a smile so radiant I'm almost ashamed. She opens the fan and flutters it gently, her eyes tracing its pattern of Oriental silk.

I'm tired, but too restless to sleep. "You know a bit about me," I say, "but I know nothing of you. Have you been at Walthingham long?"

"Yes. I left my family when I was quite young."

"Do they live close by, then?"

She folds the fan shut and tucks it out of sight in her apron. "I don't have anyone to speak of," she says. "I did have a sister once, who came with me to Walthingham Hall, but . . ." Her voice trails off, and she stretches her fingers toward the fire. "But I no longer have any family to speak of, no."

The orphan in me longs to clasp her hands, but I know such intimacy would embarrass her. I stay silent as she helps me undress. She takes such pride in folding the heavy satin, in clustering the hairpins away into a gilded box. As the clock in the hallway strikes one, she bids me good night.

Stella is already lying at the bottom of my bed, caught in a dream. I gently pat her as she paddles the air with her paws. Tonight must go down as a success in Grace's eyes, and really, I tell myself, the ball itself wasn't so bad. I think Jane and

I might become firm friends—though in truth, Elsie and I have more in common than anyone I've met since arriving at Walthingham.

I should be happy, cosseted by luxury, my every wish attended to.

I blow out the candle on the bedside table and watch the gray smoke drift.

I *should* be happy.

So why am I not?

CHAPTER 4

Dear Aunt Lila and Uncle Edward,

Your faraway girl has been a bit further than usual these days, and for that I am sincerely sorry. You mustn't believe that I've grown too grand to write; George keeps me in line quite nicely, as does the fear of using entirely the wrong utensils in front of my very high-class cousins.

I hope the winter hasn't been too harsh, and that Geoffrey has recovered from his fear of the "big horse" after his recent fall. Though I can't say I entirely blame him—Bluebell always was a cranky thing. Aunt Lila, please let me know which colors you like best, because I plan on sending you something lovely for Anna's wedding this spring.

How is Paul getting along without George to help with the horses? And how is Connor?

I pause a moment to read what I've written. After an initial flurry of homesick letters, in which I tried to portray for them the opulence of our new life, I've allowed contact with my guardians to trail off. With the time taken for the crossing, I won't hear back for many weeks anyway.

When this letter finally reaches her, will Aunt Lila show it to Connor? And if she does, will it tug at his heart just a bit, to see the paper where I've folded it, and to think of my life going on without him?

A sharp rap at the door makes me jump. The cup of hot chocolate at my elbow wobbles, but doesn't spill. Before I can answer, Grace sails in, attired for visiting. A belted salmon dress makes the most of her narrow waist, and under the wide brim of a matching hat, her face looks nearly pretty—but, as always, a bit too thin.

"I hope you slept well, cousin," she says.

"I had no choice," I say, smiling. "That mattress must be a foot deep."

In truth, my sleep was fitful, punctured with dreams as strange as the preceding events. Behind my eyelids, something paced with a heavy tread. I woke to the long, keening sound of a woman's scream—which faded to nothing as my dream deserted me.

Grace assesses me with a raised chin, as she always does, before nodding once. "You look very well," she says.

When she brought the hot chocolate, Elsie also carried in

a deep blue day dress, with a puffed bodice and split skirt revealing an underskirt of palest ivory. The days when I'd throw on the first patched dress that came to hand and keep it on until bedtime feel very far away; here there are rules even about the clothes one wears in bed.

Grace wanders over to the window.

"I've received many cards of thanks for last night's ball, and more than one contained admiring words about you, Katherine."

My cheeks redden, and she smiles, moving forward and cupping her hand beneath my chin.

"Such pretty roses," she says. "It's an accomplishment to bring color to your cheeks so easily."

At her touch, the memory of the drunken soldier's fingers at my throat ripples through me, and I close my eyes against it. Grace moves her hand from my chin to my forehead. "And now you've gone pale as can be. Katherine, do not move too frequently from the heat of the fire to the chill by the windows. It will make you ill quicker than anything."

Just then a racket of birdsong and shrieks from the distant aviary rends the air. As I hurry to the window, the distant shrilling fades into silence.

The air outside is lightly silvered with snow. Nothing stirs on the grounds or in the still woods just beyond. I wonder what startled the birds so.

Grace's voice comes sharp behind me. "Katherine."

I whirl quickly and find her clutching the necklace I wore the night before, which I'd left draped across my dressing table so it wouldn't tangle.

"These items need to be locked up," she says, then lowers her voice to a theatrical whisper as Elsie's footsteps come tripping down the hall. "No matter how close we may keep them, servants cannot be fully trusted."

I wonder if I should tell her now about the fan. She would not approve, I'm sure.

"Surely we can trust Elsie, Aunt Grace. She's been here since she was just old enough to work, has she not?"

"No matter, my dear. More than a few of my late mother's pieces have gone missing. Not even the most valuable ones, but often the prettiest. That's how you know it's a maid's fingers at work."

Arranging her hat more firmly atop her head, she goes to the door. "I'm off to visit a few friends who were not well enough for last night's ball. If I'm not back by the time you leave for London, I wish you a pleasant trip."

She says it in a way that suggests she's anything but happy I'm going to the city. Grace has repeated several times that she doesn't think London's the place for an "impressionable" young girl.

I glance at the enormous traveling case beside the bed, which Elsie helped me pack. "Thank you," I say. "I'm well prepared for every eventuality, as you can see."

As I settle back down in front of the fire, the clock in the hall strikes nine, and I resolve to give George just one more hour in bed before I wake him myself. We can't miss the midday coach from Bath if we're to make the overnight stop in Reading.

Putting my letter aside, I spend the next hour reading by the fire. We had books on the farm, but nothing like here.

The housekeeper, Mrs. Whiting, a sallow older woman with fading red hair, looked suspicious when I asked for a key to the library, but she grudgingly gave it all the same. Most of the volumes I came across were monstrously dull—collections of legal papers, or obscure histories of European culture—but among them I found the novels of Defoe and Scott.

I'm racing toward the end of *Robinson Crusoe* when the gilded grandfather clock in the hall strikes ten. Annoyed, I ring for Mr. Carrick to ask if he's seen George.

"I believe he's left for London, my lady," he says.

"Left? Without me?"

"He took breakfast early."

"But we're leaving together," I say.

Carrick frowns. "It seems that is not the case. May I help you in any other matter, my lady?"

When I shake my head, still mulling my brother's departure, Carrick swiftly takes his leave.

George isn't in his rooms. The fireplace in his bedchamber is empty, and the room is bathed in a cold gray light that makes me shiver.

Someone's walking over my grave, I think, and then close my mind to the thought. It's an old superstition, and not one that I believe in.

"Where *have* you gotten to, George?" I mutter.

I'm turning back toward the hall when I see the painting on his easel. It stops me midturn and fills me with an uneasy feeling.

The canvas is large, half-finished, and darker in every way than his usual works. I can see at once that it's a rendering of

Walthingham's wintry woods. White birches curve from a dark plane of raw ground into a foreboding sky. Shadows gather among the twisted roots of the trees. Though the canvas is dominated by trees, the roots draw the eye. I stand a moment, staring into them, as if I might find something crouching there.

The swirls of paint still look a little fresh, and I press the back of my thumbnail lightly to its surface. It gives wetly to my touch. Surely yesterday's work would be drier by now, unless . . . unless he was out painting this morning. There's little in this dark canvas that speaks of the blue I spied on his wrist last night—but for a faint daubing right in the top corner, streaked with gray, a window of sky breaking through the gloom.

My cloak, gloves, and soft boots are laid out in my dressing room, ready for the trip to London. I layer them over my dress, not bothering to call for Elsie. Of course George hasn't gone without me. Carrick must be mistaken. My brother has never been one for timekeeping, always showing up long after supper had cooled, always vague with his plans. But a sister is not a missed meal—George wouldn't just leave me behind. I bound down the stairs, Stella at my heels.

The crisped snow squeaks beneath my heels as I stride toward the stables. I can smell the horses before I see them. The familiar warmth of packed hay and the animals' big bodies always calms me, and I take a deep breath as I pass through the stable gate. I hear the faint sound of nickering—then, beneath it, something else. A woman's laughter, teasing and low.

Peeking around the corner, I see a high bale of sweet,

freshly turned hay . . . and atop it, my dressing maid, her hair falling from its bun and her arms wrapped tight around Matthew, the boy who stables our horses.

They must hear my gasp, because two faces turn toward me at once, one red and one pale as whey. Matt grabs his discarded hat from the straw, attempts the world's most sheepish bow, and flees into the nearest stall.

Elsie, not so quick, can barely meet my eyes as she stands, putting her clothes back into order. I have many long moments to inspect the stitching of my glove before she manages to speak. "Don't tell your cousin, I beg you," she whispers. "Or Mrs. Whiting. She'll send me away at once."

The housekeeper is even less tolerant of trespasses in etiquette than Grace is, and I have no doubt that Elsie's right.

"I won't tell anyone," I say. "Your secret is safe with me."

I raise my voice a bit, attempting to sound dignified. "Matthew, I'm traveling to Bath today. If you would, please have the carriage ready as soon as possible." I notice then that my brother's horse is not in his stall. "Where's Croxley?"

Matthew moves shyly back into view, peering over the stall door.

"Mr. Randolph must have taken him out. He was gone first thing."

First thing? We can't have gone to bed until one. "I hardly think my brother would have been riding in the freezing cold at dawn," I say.

"I'm afraid I wasn't here, my lady," he says. "I was polishing boots in the scullery."

The last I saw of George, he was tottering up the main staircase, clutching the banister like a man on the deck of a storm-tossed ship. And the last thing we spoke of was the trip to London, of taking it together—surely he could not have forgotten?

If I hurry, I can make the coach myself. When I catch up with him, my brother will have some explaining to do.

While Matt prepares the carriage, I walk back to the house to find John. I'll need a driver, and I'd much prefer it be someone I can talk to.

I'm halfway back when I see two men standing at the scullery door, speaking with John. There's something in their manner that makes me pause, then conceal myself in Walthingham's shadows before advancing. The pair should look comical next to each other—one tall and thin, the other short and nearly as thick around as he is tall—but their appearance does not inspire laughter. I judge them both to be in their forties, dressed in drab civilian suits of brown and black. The short man's neck overflows his collar, and the thin man has taken off his hat to reveal a bristling shaven head and small ears. They appear to have come on foot, which in these conditions strikes me as very odd indeed.

I creep closer, trailing my fingers against the rough stone wall.

"I've already told you once, and my answer will not change." The voice is John's. "The master of the house isn't in, and you have no business here until he's back."

"We'll keep coming back until we get what we came for," says the tall man, his voice perfectly even.

"You'll get exactly what you're owed," John replies. "But not while the master is away."

He means Henry, I suppose—though my brother is lord of Walthingham Hall in name, he has not yet taken over the running of the estate.

The tall man eyes John for a long moment. I think of a dog with its hackles up, deciding whether to flee or fight. Finally he drops his shoulders, then stabs a finger into John's chest. "Mark my words, man. You will be seeing us again, and sooner than you'd like." His eyes flick upward toward the house, taking it in, and then he and his silent companion trudge away. I wait until they've rounded the corner of the house before walking on. John is rehanging a shelf against the scullery wall, hammer in hand.

"Don't worry, they didn't see you," he says. His tone is familiar, as it always is when I'm unaccompanied, but there's something heavy in it today.

"Who were those men? What did they want with Henry?"

"Them? They're nobody you need worry about. Just masons, here to discuss the renovations of the west wing. Though they would do better to start chasing down payment *after* they've completed the job, I think."

The story is a likely one, but it strikes me as false. "Indeed," I say.

In half an hour, the carriage is ready and John is checking over the tackle. Two black mares, sleek and blanketed, toss their heads and snort. John is dressed in a long coat and gloves, with a flat cap pulled down over his ears. I've told him I want to visit Jane Dowling—I will not give him the opportunity to dissuade me from chasing my errant brother.

"You're sure you'll be warm enough?" he says as he helps me into the cushioned seats. Grace has insisted I bring two loose fur blankets, and I'm grateful for them.

"Enough," I say. "I already feel guilty that you'll be facing the elements while I'm tucked up in here."

"It's your place," he says simply.

The avenue from the front of the house sweeps through the forest, running along high ground. In the dip before the house, below sculpted gardens, lies the lake, glassy and still. Already I'm feeling freer, just moments away from the house and its restrictions. Through the glass at the front, I see John seated above the horses, swaying with the carriage's motion. Were I to need him, I could summon him by the bell-cord hanging close at hand. *My place*, indeed.

The rocking of the carriage has almost lulled me to sleep when a jounce over hard cobbles stirs me. We are descending toward the city. I see through the frosted glass the distant sweep of what must be the Royal Crescent, stately and ordered houses with columned porticoes bathed in sunlight. The snow on the road isn't too bad, but the clouds above are the color of lead.

Impulsively, I ring the bell, and John brings the carriage to a halt. Opening the glass panel at his back, he peers down at me. "Everything all right, my lady?"

I open the carriage door and step out. "Move up," I say, placing a foot on the mounting board.

"My lady?"

I climb up beside him, and he's forced to shuffle along the seat.

"I've never seen the Royal Crescent before," I say. "And the view's much better from up here."

He laughs, a happy, unguarded sound. "Your aunt would not approve," he says.

"We'd better not tell her, then."

With a flick of the reins, the carriage lurches off, down the wide roads leading to Bath. Below us, people are going about their business with their heads down. The snow beneath their feet is churned and dirty, and more falls in fat wet flakes from the sky.

"You're very good with the horses," I say. "Easy with them, I mean."

After a beat of silence, he responds. "Yes, I've been working with Walthingham's horses my whole life, like my father before me. It was a good place to grow up."

"And now that you're grown?" I ask. "Will you stay there?"

"I should think so," he says. "Until I marry, of course."

He sounds so certain of himself that I smile. "Ah, you have someone in mind, then?"

As soon as I've said it, I wonder if it's a clumsy question.

"There's not so much to it. It's just a matter of finding the right girl," he says, without looking at me.

The right girl. If I were still the Katherine I was in Virginia, and John a farmer's son from Paulstown—what then? Would we be like Elsie and Matt, sneaking off to the stables?

I flush, suddenly fearful that he can read my thoughts, and sit up straighter. "*I* mean to stay independent as long as I can," I say. "I don't wish to rush into a match."

A gaggle of children in scarves and hats cross the road in front of us, and John has to rein in sharply to let them pass. When we're moving once more, he seems to have lost the thread of our conversation. "We'll be at the Crescent soon," he says, nodding ahead.

"Oh, I must have misspoken. I don't wish to go to the Crescent."

"I thought you wished to visit Miss Dowling, my lady?"

"No, I won't bother her so soon after the ball," I say innocently. "I wish to go to the coaching house, where my brother would have departed from."

John frowns, and I know he isn't fooled. But, tapping the horse smartly with the reins, he does as I say. I am, after all, the lady of Walthingham Hall.

CHAPTER 5

THE COACHING HOUSE is called the King's Head, and it's a two-story half-timbered building in the center of the city, nestled among shops and stalls.

I step carefully from the carriage into ice-crusted mud.

John jumps down at my side. "I'll come in with you, my lady."

"There's no need," I reply.

A steward directs me to a room near the main entrance, where a portly man is filling in a ledger behind a desk. He takes off his cap as I enter.

"Can I help you, miss?" he says.

I start to explain my predicament—that I'm looking to find the whereabouts of my brother, that I, too, should have been in the midday coach—when he holds up a meaty hand to interrupt me.

"The coach couldn't go today, miss," he says. "Not with the snow."

"Oh," I say. "Then perhaps my brother went by a different route."

"No coaches today at all," he says. "It would be madness in these conditions."

"You're sure my brother's horse is not stabled here? His name is Croxley. The horse, that is. A mahogany stallion."

He glares at me above his eyeglasses, causing his chins to squash together impressively. "Quite sure, young lady. Now if you'll excuse me." He goes back to his ledger, paying me no further mind.

I leave the room, more troubled than before. If George isn't in London, where can he be? What if he went out to paint and got lost in the woods? What if his horse slipped and . . . I shake my head sharply. I won't let myself get carried away. He's probably back at the house already, feet up, snug and warm. He's going to laugh at me when I get home, blue with cold. *You should have left a note*, I'll tell him. That will only make him laugh more.

I'm walking back to my carriage when a man beside a piebald stallion catches my eye. His shoulders are broad beneath a crisp black coat, and the wind has ruffled his dark hair into disarray. He says something I can't hear to the steward beside him, and they both laugh.

With a start of recognition, I realize that it's William Simpson—a man I hardly imagined capable of laughter. Beneath his open coat, he wears a dark suit with a buttoned waistcoat. When our eyes meet, I raise a gloved hand to greet him. His smile falters, and he gazes at me with surprise, and something else. Disappointment? Red color rushes into his pale cheeks as I walk determinedly toward him.

"Lady Katherine," he says, with a small bow. "What are you doing here?"

His tone is faintly accusing.

"Mr. Simpson. How lovely to see you, too. I was looking for my brother."

He lifts an eyebrow. "That makes two of us."

"I beg your pardon?"

Mr. Simpson clutches a document case in one hand, and gestures to the coaching house with the other. "We were supposed to travel together to London," he says.

"*You* were going with him?"

Mr. Simpson nods briskly. "He wanted someone to find him an agent in London, to arrange the sale of his paintings."

"George never told me that," I say, in a more accusing tone than I intended.

He bristles. "That is between you and your brother," he says.

"And why didn't you say anything last night?" I ask him playfully. "As I recall, we were looking at a painting together at Walthingham Hall." I want to make him smile again, the way he did for the steward.

"There was no opportunity," he says, and judging from his pained expression, I know he is remembering his hurried exit. This isn't going well at all. "Perhaps you think I'm ill suited to the task?" he persists. "Though I may be just a lawyer, I'm not entirely unschooled in the sale of art."

"No, of course not. That isn't what I—"

"No matter," says Mr. Simpson. "The coach was canceled

in any case, and Lord Walthingham never arrived. When you see him next, do tell him that I'll be waiting on him here until the roads clear."

He nods to the steward, and walks back toward the coaching house.

The snow thickens as we make our way back through the countryside, and my unhappiness deepens with it. It's too cold to sit up beside John, and he answers my misery with a tactful silence.

My anger at George for being so inconsiderate mixes in my mind with frustration at Mr. Simpson's paranoid sensitivity. He *must* have a sense of humor, however deeply buried.

It's not long before we're cresting the final ridge before the estate's borders, and Walthingham's great facade becomes visible in the distance. Though it's beautiful, its pale stone and glass illuminated in the dying light, it looks cold. The unlit windows of the upper floors peer at me like empty eyes.

Suddenly, one of the horses whinnies and the carriage lists sharply to the left. I brace myself against the door as we clatter sideways across the road, finally bumping to a heavy halt against a copse of bare trees.

"Are you all right back there, my lady?"

"Yes, I'm fine!" I call. I fumble with the door at my back until it swings open, then climb carefully out. Were it summer, I imagine I could look straight up into an acre of green-golden leaves; as it is, the carriage rests among black brambles clustered around the sturdy trunks of ancient, snow-silvered oaks.

John's already moved toward the horses, pushing his face into theirs, crooning quiet things to keep them calm. "We've lost a wheel, my lady," he says. "Get back inside and keep as warm as you can. I'll go to the house and get help."

"I'll come with you," I say.

"No," he says firmly. Am I mistaken, or does he cast a nervous glance toward the forest? "What I mean is, His Lordship would have my guts for garters should anything happen to you. It's a cold slog up to the house from here."

I've walked miles in worse, but that's when I was just Katherine. "Very well," I say heavily, stepping back onto the mounting board.

I settle back into my crooked seat as John strides up the track. Sitting among my fur blankets, I'm overcome with self-pity. What a wretched end to a wretched day.

As my ears get used to the quiet, I notice the noises of the forest—faint crackles and snaps in the frigid air. The horses stamp their feet to stay warm, and I try to judge the time by the darkening sky.

Despite the furs, cold seeps into my toes and fingertips. Ten minutes pass—perhaps fifteen—before I notice that I can see my breath. How long could it take John to get to the house and back? Surely he should have returned by now.

Unless something has happened to him on the way. I peer through the window at the dark forest. The Beast is a myth, I remind myself—but what if John has stumbled and hurt himself? Or what if he came across a poacher?

Time stretches, out here in the snow. Flakes fall and vanish on the horses' backs, poor things. Their manes are tinged with white. I've learned over long Virginia winters to be wary about frostbite, and to watch for the moment when chilly wakefulness turns into dreamy fatigue. When I start to feel warm again, I know it's a bad thing. I clap my hands against my arms, stamp my feet to wake my legs. This won't do. I can't just wait to freeze.

So I climb out, lifting my heavy skirts clear of the snow's crust. I unhitch both horses and throw the blankets over their broad backs. It's been a little while since I rode bareback, and the larger of the mares stumbles a bit as I mount her, eyes rolling whitely in her head.

"Let's just take this slowly," I mutter.

I trot her up the track toward the house, leading the other horse close beside us. I daren't risk going any faster for fear of the ice that might be hidden beneath the snow.

Finally, frustrated by our slow progress, I lead the horses off the uneven road and down toward the lake. It's a quicker route, and the ground is softer. According to Henry, the lake was dug by our great-great-grandfather, to make the most of the tributary of the River Avon, which runs through the estate. My own grandfather constructed the elegant Palladian bridge that spans its center in a gentle arch. When I first saw it, I thought it was the most beautiful thing I'd ever laid eyes on.

There's a cruel beauty to the landscape. I think, not for the first time, how much I wish to see my new home in summer. "Maybe I could love it then," I whisper, not knowing I'm speaking aloud until the words are already said.

The lake is set like a geode into the snow, its icy black center lapping against the hard-set crystals at its shallow edges. The horses, for some reason, don't want to cross. I nudge the mare harder, and she gives in, taking tentative steps up onto the bridge. The house is just two hundred yards up the lawn now. Nearly there.

We're halfway across when a flapping of wings startles the horses.

A patch of the lake near its center teems with crows. Shabby in their black overcoats, they pick at its surface, like vultures scavenging for carrion. I gaze down at them, and then freeze. My eyes grow hot in my skull, and my fingers clench tighter on the reins.

Because now I can see that the crows are concealing something with their raggedy bodies. Something dark and unrecognizable, half-frozen into the ice. I dismount and, at the same time, see three figures speeding toward me from the house. It's John and Mr. Carrick and Henry. Not George. My brother isn't with them.

Horror steals over my heart as I move my gaze back to the lake.

It cannot be.

On the bank is an overturned boat, just a small thing for an oarsman and a single passenger. It's tied to a jetty by a thick rope caked in snow. I leave the horses whickering on the bridge.

John has broken into a run, away from the others, his feet kicking up snow as he descends. He's shouting something— my name, I think.

It cannot be.

I hook my fingers beneath the boat and heave it over. The rope is stiff as I unhook it from the mooring post. With a push, the boat slides from the bank and settles on the water, sending a ripple cracking through the ice.

Then John is at my side, his arm around my shoulder.

"Lady Katherine," he says, "please."

I point speechlessly at the water, to the thing half-submerged in the grip of the ice. The crows screech at one another, hopping and swooping in their attempts to get closer to it.

"It's just a deer, my lady," says John. "They sometimes fall in when they try to drink. . . ." His voice breaks off, ragged.

And now I know for sure.

"What's happening down there?" calls Henry. He's moving more quickly now, pulling his bad leg through the snow.

I tug myself from John's side and steady myself against the boat. Icy water pools around my boots as I climb inside. John follows wordlessly. He turns out the oars tucked into the boat's sides and, with strong strokes, propels us through jellied black ice.

Henry calls to us from the shore, a single word that I don't hear. I motion for John to row on, until we're close enough to scare off the crows. He drops the oars with a clank into the rowlocks and pulls at my arm, trying to turn me around. "Don't look."

His voice is taut, made to be obeyed, but it's too late. The body, in dark, waterlogged velvet, is facedown and still, but the hair crawls with faint, underwater currents. One hand taps noiselessly against the ice.

On its wrist is a stripe of cerulean blue.

CHAPTER 6

I FEEL WONDERFULLY WARM, and my head no longer aches. I float blissfully in the dark, my limbs loose and lazy. But as much as I try to ignore it, there's something terrible pacing at the edges of my mind, looking for a way in. I turn my head from it, again and again, but I'm waking up now, and finally it claws its way into my consciousness. . . .

"Let her sleep now."

It's Grace's voice. Remembering that my brother is dead is a duller pain than I would've thought. It turns my body to wood; I can't believe that I will ever raise my head again. My eyes are sandpaper, too dry to open, until the tears start to fall. I'm doing nothing—not really crying, even—but they're coming as regularly as rain, and I let them well through my eyelids and onto my cheeks.

When a stifled sob breaks out of me, Grace and Elsie are

on me in a flash, each taking a hand from either side of the couch they've laid me across. "Oh, Lady Katherine," Elsie begins, then bursts into tears. She pulls her apron to her face. Grace dismisses her with a weary wave, and she runs from the room.

With every beat of my heart, my grief deepens. I'm alone here. My brother, my laughing brother, is dead. No more paintings. No more George. Nobody to call me Wildcat.

I pull at my clothes, gasping, suddenly unable to breathe, and Grace brings a sharp-smelling vial to my nose, followed by a short belt of brown liquid in a cut crystal tumbler. "This will help get you through until Dr. Ebner arrives," she says, helping me to sit up.

The burning in my nose and at the back of my throat distracts me briefly from my misery. When the door shushes open a moment later, it's with an apologetic air, bringing to mind the days that followed my parents' deaths. Everyone around George and me moved in slow motion, as though we couldn't handle sharp movements. I'd felt like I was underwater.

A man in a tweed waistcoat enters the room, carrying a black leather medical bag. He's followed by Stella and an ice-pale Jane. I wonder how long I've been unconscious, that she's been fetched already from Bath. Stella kicks about the room, pleased to see me, but Grace blocks her from jumping on the couch. I want to tell her to put Stella in my arms, but the doctor has already sat down and taken my hand.

"I'm deeply sorry, Lady Randolph," he says, his mouth just discernible beneath a bushy gray mustache. His brows droop over whiskey-brown eyes, and I think how much George would like to paint a face like this. George, George, George. Every moment I remember it afresh, and it's another stab to my chest.

He places a careful hand to my brow. "Can you stand, my lady? I'm afraid you'll become overheated. Walk a moment, catch your breath."

I stand on yearling's legs. Just beyond the window, the men carry something between them, unwieldy and wrapped in sodden white. I count four bowed heads around my brother's body: Henry and John, Matt and Mr. Carrick.

"Where are they taking him?" I ask, my voice cracking and hoarse.

Grace shakes her head, just barely, but the doctor ignores her. "They're taking him to the west wing. It's the coldest part of the house, you see." He stops uncomfortably, but I take his meaning, knowing they must keep his body from the heat.

"What a terrible, terrible thing," Grace says in a sodden voice. She sits down heavily. "We will build up the railing on the bridge immediately." She turns her pale face to me. "Forgive me, Katherine, that this accident happened at Walthingham Hall!"

"An accident," I parrot dumbly. "But . . . but George was a strong swimmer. He could swim before he could walk. Even if he slipped . . ."

A memory of George as a boy, diving into the ice-cold creek with Connor, threatens to overwhelm me.

Jane moves forward, silhouetted against the fire's glow. "It doesn't matter in such cold water, Kat. Nobody could swim across that lake in winter. It would stop his heart."

I turn my face away just as Henry enters the room, trailed by John. Henry moves to my side with speed, which suits me better than the slow, skittish movements more usual to mourning. Laying a heavy hand on my shoulder, he kneels beside me with moist eyes. His skin is sickly pale.

"Oh, my sweet cousin," he says. "You can't know how sorry I am."

"He couldn't just drown, Henry," I say. "He couldn't have."

The doctor moves toward us, uneasy, and Henry looks at me sadly. "There is no other explanation, Katherine. A young man at his first ball, on unfamiliar grounds. And he'd had a bit to drink. . . ."

I clutch at his arm. "But he rode to Bath," I say. "Matt said his horse was gone first thing."

Henry shares a look with Grace.

"What is it?" I say.

Henry clears his throat. "Croxley came back to the stables an hour ago. He was cold with wandering, but Matt's seen him right."

I fall back against the couch, shaking my head.

"He must have thrown your brother on that bridge before running off," Henry continues. "He could be wild, that one. He damn near toppled me once."

Grace *tsks* her tongue at the profanity, and in the hush that follows, all eyes watch me with unspoken pity. Except John, who lowers his gaze. Dr. Ebner rattles through his medical bag before producing a small bottle of something that I can tell will be sickly sweet just by looking at it.

"I will examine your brother's body, Lady Randolph," he

says, "to determine whether it was the fall or the water that killed him. But you mustn't trouble yourself with such unsavory things. It's imperative that you take something to calm your nerves."

My energy spent, I allow him to administer the syrupy medicine. Grace asks him in quiet tones whether the body must truly be examined, and Henry retreats to the fire, to stand close by Jane.

The room seems suddenly terribly full with people. As the medicine takes effect, my mind grows fuzzy at the edges. I sense more than see John steal toward me, and then cover me with his coat. Its familiar smell of horses and wintry air fills me with such grief I feel weak.

As I drift into sleep, I hear two servants by the fire, speaking low. "You won't catch me going outside after dark again," one mutters. "Not now that the Beast of Walthingham has claimed another."

I'm alone now even in my sleep, too drugged and exhausted for dreams. When I wake, it's still dark. Clutching for John's coat, I find the silken coverlet of my own bed. Someone's carried me upstairs and stripped me down to my smallclothes.

By the fire's dying glow, I can make out a sleeping shape on a chair next to the bed. My heart expands—then contracts like a fist when I see that it's too small to be a man. After a moment I understand that it's Jane. Stella, splayed across her lap, rouses for a moment, then twitches back into sleep.

My mind flies to my brother, lying in cold solitude at the far end of the house. Can he really be gone? It seems impossible. A cavernous loneliness yawns below me as I shift to sitting, shivering despite the closeness of the air.

I shroud myself tightly in a trailing blanket and steal from the stifling room, pinching at the ache between my eyes. Silently I make my way toward the west wing, averting my gaze from the door that leads to my brother's former chambers. I've only ever seen the damaged wing from the grounds. A hastily built temporary wall separates it from the rest of the house; when I unlock the workmen's door and step over the threshold, drafts bite at my skin.

Moonlight through uncurtained windows illuminates sheet-covered shapes and shining patches of incongruously ornate wooden floors. There's a slight scuttling sound in the walls; I pause a moment, and it fades away. After a few wrong doors, I find my way to George, laid out in a small parlor.

They've placed him on a high, spare table, so perfectly suited for his long shape that I can't imagine what use it had before this. I drop my blanket and move to his side. The house breathes around us, full of silent, sleeping life, and I can't stand the thought that George alone will never wake.

My daredevil brother thought himself invincible, it's true. He was known to ride without a saddle, to dive into shady pools without checking their depth, to wander too close to animal dens in pursuit of the perfect vantage for painting. But he was no fool. Why would he ride in bad light on an icy bridge?

Breathing in through my mouth, I peel the sheet away.

His body inspires no horror in me, just a great, bottomless pity. I've seen death many times before. I even found a body in the river once in Virginia, in high summer. The man was a drifter we never identified, bloated beyond all recognition.

I make myself look at my brother, clenching my chattering teeth. His skin looks gray in the moonlight, his features unrecognizable. I can hardly bear to see his elegant, able hands, now swollen and still. Only his hair is the same, fluffy and fine. I touch it tenderly, pushing it back from his brow—and see a livid gash, running from his temple and up along his hairline.

The wound is long and deep. When I was small, the youngest girl on the Andersen farm was found among the blackberry bushes on her father's land, nearly dead after being mauled by a bear. She survived, but her hair never grew straight along the left side of her scalp, and her forehead was permanently scarred.

George's wound looks something like hers—something like the track of an animal's claw. I lean in closer, holding my breath. *The Beast of Walthingham preys on the wicked, they say.* . . .

Suddenly, the room dances with light. I throw the sheet back over George's face and spin around, breathing fast. John stands in the doorway, holding a lantern high. His arm is trembling, making the lamplight skitter crazily across the walls. I snatch my blanket from the floor and fold it around my shivering body.

His mouth is a heavy line, the sockets of his eyes hollowed and strange. For a moment I'm frightened, but then he lowers the lamp, and the shadows retreat. He's clad only in breeches and a loose nightshirt, his hair tousled with sleep.

"Lady Katherine. I worried when I heard someone walking

about." He looks no less troubled now, running his eyes over me in the dim light. "You should go to bed, my lady," he says finally. "The west wing is far from secure."

He falls silent as I step closer. "John," I say. "Please. Please tell me what you know about the Beast of Walthingham." My voice crackles over the words, and his face goes gentle.

"My lady," he says, "I know nothing, because there's nothing to know. The Beast is a fairy tale."

"But there's *something* in that forest, isn't there? Something the servants are frightened of."

"The tales of scullery maids don't hold much water, miss."

And yet he's hiding something, I'm sure of it.

"But if there's something to it, anything, you must tell me. This is my home. And I saw something yesterday evening, at the edge of the woods. A man, perhaps . . ."

John shrugs. "Big estates like this, they attract poachers. Locals looking for food. There's no point trying to drive them off; the forest's too big."

"Then a poacher may have done this to my brother."

"I did not mean to say . . . I did not try to imply that your brother was killed. It was, as your cousin said, a terrible accident."

"I don't believe it." As I say the words, I know they're true. The pain behind my eyes spreads.

John dips his head low and looks into my eyes. "Don't open your heart to pain that has no place there. Your brother's loss alone will hurt enough. There's nobody to blame, nobody to hate."

"You're wrong," I say hotly. "The pain will ease some, if there's somebody to blame. Somebody to punish."

His eyes are startled at this, and he reaches out a careful hand, places it lightly on my shoulder. I grow still beneath the touch.

"There will always be poachers on these large estates, but few of them are murderers, too." He drops his hand back to his side. "Poachers will exist for as long as the poor need to eat and maintain their desire to get back at the rich. That is to say, forever." There's an edge in his voice that is new.

"Don't speak to me of vendettas now, when my brother is barely cold," I say, angry. "If he could, he would remind you that the rules of decency extend to both rich and poor. I should know—I'm newly rich, and very recently was quite poor. But I'm the same person now that I was then."

John reaches a hand toward mine and takes it, his fingertips gently insistent on my palm. "Are you, my lady?" His voice is husky, with a texture in it that I've never heard.

Though the room is frigid, my skin is suddenly alive with heat, running in currents from my palm all the way to my scalp.

"You're shivering," he says. "Are you cold?"

I nod but cannot speak, watching his chest rise and fall in the half-light. His skin is ruddy with beating blood, and I long to feel the life of him in my arms. Almost without my permission, my face is moving toward his.

Then another, steadier light joins that of John's lamp, and I hear Jane's voice, tentative, from the hall. "Katherine?" she says. John has already moved away from me, slipping like a phantom through a side door, deeper into the abandoned wing.

Jane enters the room, clutching a candle and a subdued

Stella. "You weren't in bed when I woke," she says, her voice a colorless slip. "I was so worried, Kat."

Her eyes fall on my brother's sheeted form. "Oh. Of course. I'm so sorry. I should have known you would want to see him."

She won't look directly at me, and I wonder how much she saw of John and me before calling out my name. As she leads me back to my room, I cannot decide whether I'm grateful for the way she interrupted us, just before my mouth touched his.

CHAPTER 7

Despite everything, the procedures must be followed. I stand in front of the mirror once more, this time dressed in black. "I'm not sure I can do this," I say, trying to avoid my reflection. "Face all those people."

Jane smiles wanly. She, too, is dressed for the funeral, her clothes having been brought to the house in preparation. "Would you like me to tell them you are unwell?" she says.

It would hardly be a lie. My skin is so pale, my eye sockets shrunken and bruised through troubled sleep. I want to lie on my bed and close my eyes and simply forget—to drift on a sea of unconsciousness. Perhaps I will, by some miracle, open them again and find myself back in our old house, with Aunt Lila singing in the kitchen, and the thud of Connor and George chopping wood outside.

"No," I say. "I owe it to him to go."

Tears are brimming again, and Jane wraps her arms around me, letting me shudder silently. After the fit has passed, she offers me a cloth to dab my eyes. "It is not the same," she says, "but I know something of grief. It's three years since my mother passed."

"I'm sorry," I say.

"Don't be," Jane answers. "I have only happy memories of her. She was a kind woman, with a generous spirit. Just like your brother, from what I knew of him. I cannot offer you much consolation, but know this. Time will soften your grief."

I touch her shoulder lightly. "Thank you." Glancing at the clock, I see it is almost eleven. "We should go downstairs."

She takes my arm, just as George did the night before he died. We descend the stairs to the front of the house, where Grace and Henry wait with the two mourning coaches. Mr. Dowling is there also, in his own transport. Henry's face is drawn beneath his hat. There's a patch of dried blood below his ear, where he's cut himself shaving.

Only the sight of John, driving a second coach, shakes me from my dulled reverie. Though he can't bring his eyes to mine, I know he sees me. I mean to catch him alone, to tell him that our near-kiss was a foolish thing, that it mustn't be repeated.

"You look splendid," said Grace, admiring the outfit she herself picked out for me.

Carrick stands aside and offers an arm to help me into the carriage, but I pause. "Perhaps Jane and I could travel alone, in the second?" I ask, nodding toward John's carriage.

Grace bristles. "That wouldn't be . . ."

"Of course, cousin," says Henry quickly. "We will see you at the church,"

Jane goes to her father and he nods kindly at me. Taking his seat alongside his driver, he leaves the carriage for Jane and me. As the horses' hooves click, I lean back and breathe a sigh. A few more moments alone will help me compose myself.

Walthingham has a chapel of its own, and I would have preferred to say farewell within that private space, but Henry has said it would be inappropriate with so many others wishing to pay their condolences to my dead brother. Why, I do not know. No one here truly knew him.

The church is a narrow gray building with a single spire. We disembark at the gate and join the small gathering of gentry wending their way toward my family's tomb.

I keep my face impassive and my neck held straight beneath the heavy black bonnet, and turn my mourning ring inward until its beveled enamel bites into my palm. The flash of pain keeps me from drooping into despair before this sea of curious eyes.

More people even than attended our ball have turned out to observe the sudden passing of George Randolph, the new heir of Walthingham. Here and there I see a face I recognize from that glittering night. Lady Flint, looking sallower than ever in starched black. The first man that I danced with, sitting ill at ease with his fellow soldiers. And the woman who wore green satin and made me believe that something vicious stalked the grounds at Walthingham. Her son is beside her, but he won't meet my eyes.

Though they're here as mourners, these people seem more

interested in gawking at my clothing than in paying tribute to George. And Grace has made certain that I'm worth staring at. My hastily bought mourning clothes include a Russian wrapping-cloak, worn open over a crepe-trimmed black column. The toes of black leather boots peep out below, and I clutch a reticule frothy with lace.

I hate my finery, and even more, I hate Grace's insistence that I perform this show of grieving for the sake of people I hardly know, who hardly knew George. She insists that I honor my dead in the *proper* way, but proper to me is how we observed my parents' passing: two pine boxes, prayers as they were lowered into the earth. We wore dark colors but could not take more than half a day away from the farm. Hard work distracted and healed us, slowly. Here there is nothing to carry my mind from my loss. Just dressing and undressing, broken sleep and grief-shadowed waking hours.

I bring my hand in its dull black glove to the silver filigree brooch at my neck, wound round with a lock of my brother's hair. Grace keeps her head bowed and her arm through her brother's. Though they're not visibly close, not like George and I were, I still feel the beginnings of pity as I contemplate what will happen to her once Henry marries Jane. Women are useless enough among the rich, and unmarried women even more so.

Jane begins to move away, but I cling to her. "Please, stay with me," I say. Grace again looks a little confused, but I avoid her gaze.

The wind blows bitterly as we cross the frozen ground, and the air tastes burnt and thin. George will be buried here, beside our grandfather, instead of with our parents in the rich soil of home. His body will never be joined by that of a wife, or a child. Perhaps my own will join his, one day, should I die unmarried. Jane and I stand at the graveside together, our two bonnets bowed side by side.

The priest's words, consigning my brother to the Lord, are nearly lost to the wind whistling around the headstones. The service is nothing but impersonal verses, suitable for the passing of any stranger, and I feel a cool numbness as it nears its end.

Then a low ripple of unease runs through the gathered mourners, and Jane's hand tightens on my arm. I follow her gaze across the grounds. The sunlight on snow is blinding, but I can still see the strange man approaching, picking his way toward us from the other side of the churchyard.

He's tall and whippet-thin, wearing a patched black jacket and a cap pulled tight over his ears. When he gets closer I judge that he's sixty at least, his face brown and sun-weathered. His eyes under sharp brows are too bright. Though he pulls off his cap with a clumsy hand as he draws near, squeezing it into a ball, the brightness of his darting eyes makes him look disrespectful all the same.

The other guests have noticed him, and some are rudely whispering to their companions. Even Henry is standing up straight, his mouth tight.

I look at Jane, whose face shows recognition and alarm.

Then the men begin to lower George into the earth, and the stranger is briefly forgotten. The pallbearers grunt softly as they ease him down, and I feel a wave of pain so disorienting that Jane must help me stand. And then it's over; he's disappeared below the lip of the frozen ground, and I'm the only Randolph left.

When I look up, my eyes streaming hot tears, the old man is looking straight at me. I meet his glare until Henry passes between us, leaving Grace's side to stride over to the stranger.

"How dare you show your face here?" Henry's voice carries on the frozen air, sharp and shocking. "This is a family affair, and I won't have you disrespecting that."

The man's piercing eyes have gone cold, with a hatred I can discern even from where I stand. For a moment I wonder whether he'll strike Henry, but finally he raises his chin and speaks. "A family affair, you say?" Pointedly he sweeps his gaze over the multitude of indifferent aristocrats stamping their chilly feet around my brother's grave. "I served Walthingham Hall near as many years as you've been alive, boy. I mean to pay my respects, the same as anyone else."

"Your respects are neither asked for nor accepted. You're not welcome here, or anywhere on my grounds."

The man looks at Henry for a moment, and then gives a short, sharp laugh that shrivels my breath. He leans into my cousin's ear and begins to speak, too quietly for me to hear. Henry's face is turned from mine, but I see his body go utterly still as he listens. His fists start to tighten. . . .

Then John charges across the snow, putting his body between them. "Leave it, McAllister," he says, throwing a restraining arm across the old man's chest. "This is not the day to speak of old grievances." Keeping a grip on his arm, John walks him away from the service, and from my angry cousin.

Henry still stands rigid on the snow when Mr. Dowling approaches me, gently taking my arm. "I regret this interruption to your brother's service, my lady. You should not have to deal with these things while you're grieving."

"Who is that man?"

"He was once your grandfather's gamekeeper, until he was discovered selling Walthingham's stock for his own gain." There's something like pity in his voice as he continues. "A man like that could only end up a poacher, of course, especially with no good reference."

"He's a poacher?" I say, closing my eyes briefly and remembering the dark shape at the edge of the trees. What if, on George's last morning, he had come across this angry man in Walthingham's woods?

Mr. Dowling coughs lightly. "One of many. A place like Walthingham will always attract his sort."

By now McAllister has wrenched himself from John's grip and is disappearing down the road from the church. In his anger he bumps into someone coming from the opposite direction; it's a moment before I recognize the man as William Simpson. He and McAllister lock eyes for a long moment, though neither speaks. Then, with a sharp bob of his head, the poacher continues on his way.

Mr. Dowling politely removes himself and Jane goes with him as Mr. Simpson walks toward me, pulling off his hat. As he squints down at me, our cold exchange in Bath seems to belong to another lifetime. I realize I'm happy to see him.

"May I speak to you a moment, Lady Randolph?" he says softly, looking into my face.

Grace is hovering behind me; I give her a small nod and step toward him. "Yes, of course. I'm glad you're here."

"I wish that it were under any other circumstance," he says. "I deeply regret this loss. I spoke glibly of his disappearance when I last saw you, and I must beg you to forgive me."

"We were both speaking under a misapprehension that day."

He nods soberly. "May we speak in private?"

Grace is now occupied with another mourner, and I take the opportunity to tuck my arm in his. "Of course."

He stiffens a moment under my touch, then relaxes. We walk in silence over the swell of the path. I run my eyes across gravestone etchings clotted with snow, looking away quickly when I see the headstones of children. DEAREST BELOVED, reads one, in blocky script. Even before my parents' deaths I was frightened of cemeteries.

When my cousins and their companions are faraway shapes, Mr. Simpson stops, gently disengaging his arm from mine. He waits a discreet moment, then speaks. "My lady, it is important that we discuss a great many things. You must understand the full extent of your inheritance, now that you are the sole heir of Walthingham."

The words hit me like a cold gust. "I . . . had not thought of it that way," I stammer. The heir of Walthingham?

"It's a privilege, and a grave responsibility," he persists. "Though my timing may seem importunate, we must speak of certain matters . . ."

Irritation flares up in me, making my stomach sour. "Yes, your timing does seem *importunate*, Mr. Simpson. You truly wish me to discuss business and legal details with you now? On this very day?"

"I have the greatest sympathy for your situation, but this is something that cannot wait for long. As your brother's untimely passing has made clear, it's important that your affairs are always in order. You will one day be mistress of one of the finest houses in England."

His chiding tone falls heavy on my ears, making me shrink back inside of myself. "I'm certain you are an excellent lawyer, one whose affairs are never out of line. But your talk of responsibility brings me no comfort today. I'll thank you to leave my affairs well alone."

"But your grandfather's legacy . . ."

"*I* am my grandfather's legacy, sir. The legacy of a man who drove away his only son: a stranger to my grandfather, a stranger to England. You ask me to be grateful for my inheritance, but to me it is only a burden, a gift from a dying man who saw his folly too late." My breath is coming fast and sharp, with a rising tide of anger I barely knew I harbored. "My brother's death was no accident, I'm sure of it, and it never would have happened if we hadn't come here. He should be safely in Virginia even now. As should I."

Mr. Simpson is looking down at his hands; in regret or disappointment, I cannot tell. "You mustn't speak that way of Lord Walthingham. He could not have known; he could not have foreseen . . ."

"I *will not* speak of this today. I will not speak to *you* today. Please don't approach me about the estate again, until my period of mourning has ended."

I turn from him before he can see the tears springing to my eyes, letting the wind dry them as I speed back toward my brother's resting place. I look back once, but Mr. Simpson does not see me. He's standing where I left him, straight-backed and still in the snowy churchyard.

CHAPTER 8

T HE MOURNERS GATHERED around Henry and Grace mutter insincere condolences with artfully pitying eyes, their avid faces barely concealed by the black brims of their hats. I accept the limp-fingered comfort of several ladies in fashionable black, dabbing their eyes with ornamental handkerchiefs.

John is standing by the imposing stone crypt that houses my grandfather's coffin and those of other, long-gone Randolphs. When I see him, the shame of what nearly happened last night makes my stomach twist. I'm suddenly anxious to put an end to it, to whatever he might think there is between us. I can put that to rights today, at least.

His face as I approach is sad and weary, fixed intently on the crypt. I'm surprised to see it, and wonder whether he was fond of my grandfather—John did, after all, grow up on the estate. My anger at the former Lord Walthingham seems foolish now. He and his sins are dead and buried, and my brother keeps him company in the earth.

Even when I've reached John's side, he does not look up at me. I follow his gaze to the stone and read the inscription there. *He watches over us all. In memoriam.* "It's a little somber, don't you think?" I say.

John shrugs. "I don't know the last word," he says. "My letters aren't good."

"It's 'memoriam,'" I say casually, so as not to make him feel foolish. "It just means 'memory.'"

John nods. "It was your grandfather who taught me my first letters," he says. "Gave me one of the books from his library—one that Mr. Campion himself studied as a boy."

"And now?" I ask. "Do you still read?"

A blush rises to John's cheeks. "No, my lady. Not anymore."

His tone is underlined with finality. I can't imagine Grace or Henry offering John access to the library, but I make a mental note to speak to them about it.

"Do you believe that, my lady?" John asks, turning his eyes on mine with unexpected urgency. "Do you believe that the dead watch us still, and . . . and can see all that we do?"

"I don't think of it like that, exactly. I don't *really* think that George can see me. Or my parents, either." I duck my head and will back the tears waiting just behind my eyes. Then I feel John's hand reach for mine and clasp it, under my cloak. I'm so shocked by the gesture that it takes a moment for me to notice the way the steady warmth of his touch takes the raw edges off the cold. Every moment, I think that I should pull away, but I don't.

"My lady," he says, his voice low. "I am so very sorry for your loss." He squeezes my hand gently, then releases it and walks away. But I detect a disturbance in his step, the same confused tremor that runs through me now, carrying some current of lightness into my heart.

I call out his name without thinking, and when he turns I can't imagine what I meant to tell him. "John," I say. "John. Let me teach you how to read better. I fear you're missing out." It's all I can think to offer.

"I would like that," he says, smiling. He drops into a quick bow, then walks back toward the carriage.

My heart beats easier now, until I turn and lock eyes with Grace. She's watching me from the windbreak beside the far church wall, her eyes nearly lost in shadow. She holds my gaze for half a moment, and then turns away, tipping her face up toward the sun. Her closed eyes and drawn mouth give no hint of just how much she saw.

On the ride home, I press my forehead to the cool of the carriage window. Henry contrived somehow to ride with Jane, and now I am squeezed rather uncomfortably across the bench with both Grace and Mr. Dowling. "Of course I'm very pleased with the attendance today, very pleased indeed," she tells him with great satisfaction, as if George's funeral were no different from any successful ball. She repeats the flattering comments made by her friends, on George and myself, and on her own tasteful mourning clothes. My head hurts to hear it, but Mr. Dowling is a gentleman. He behaves as though her every observation is fascinating and correct.

The house as we approach looks desolate, though the windows are lit. I wonder whether they've closed up George's rooms yet, and what will happen to all his fine new things. Most of his clothing he never got the chance to wear, and the old things have surely been spirited away by Grace and Mr. Carrick to some unvisited corner of the house.

Jane and Henry made better time and are waiting outside for us when we arrive. Her cheeks are flushed, his eyes particularly bright; I wonder what passed between them on the ride. In the flurry of our arrival, I take hold of Henry's arm, letting the rest of them walk ahead of us into the house.

When I'm sure they're out of earshot, I speak to him from the corner of my mouth. "Henry, I *must* talk to you, somewhere I might not upset Jane and Grace."

He nods slightly and asks no questions, guiding me into an antechamber off the main parlor. The room is cold, and thick with the incongruous scent of hothouse flowers. Grace has ordered them to be placed in every room, and I think I will never love the scent of roses again. Henry, too, wrinkles his nose as I turn to face him.

"Henry, do you believe in the Beast of Walthingham?"

Though he looks surprised, his response is fast and firm. "Absolutely not, Katherine. I regret that the tale was ever spoken of in your presence."

"Then if there is no Beast," I persist, "you must listen to me when I say that George's fall was not an accident. I saw his body, Henry, the night after we found him. His forehead was badly cut. If he drowned, there's no reason for him to have such a wound. Something else happened to him—something else made him fall!"

I feel my words getting wilder, but I can't help myself. Henry leads me to a blue brocade sofa, punctuated with hard black buttons. "Katherine, please sit, before you upset yourself."

It strikes me suddenly that I can't stand the useless furniture of the rich, and I push his arm aside. "I don't want to sit. I want to talk to the magistrate!"

"Mr. Dowling will be happy to speak with you," Henry says calmly, "but I fear for you, Katherine, in this state. All the roses have gone from your cheeks!"

"I'm not a foolish child," I say sharply. "You must think more highly of me than that, cousin."

His face is suddenly grave, all its forced jocularity fled. "You're right, Katherine. You've lost too many loved ones to have the luxury of being childish, and I'm very sorry for it." He moves to a cabinet of lacquered wood topped with a carved checkerboard. Balanced carefully on his injured leg, he crouches before it. There's a cunning catch somewhere on the cabinet's side; when he presses it, the door swings open, revealing a silver tray cluttered with bottles, some of them conspicuously low.

"I'll fix you something that will knock some heat back into you, at any rate—it worked for me in France; it will work for you in England. So long as you don't share my recipe with anyone—especially my sister."

Defeated, I drop onto an ornate carved chair to watch him work. The draft he mixes is spiced and syrupy, with an astringent kick that clears my head.

"You learned this recipe on the battlefield, did you?" I say.

"I did. More often than not, our battles were fought against boredom. At times we could almost forget we were at war, passing our time as we did with card games and attempts to keep warm from the inside out." He ruefully holds up his drink. "Those quiet times never lasted for long, of course—we were always reminded soon enough of why we were there. The luxury of Walthingham seemed a beautiful dream to me, one I longed to return to, but the men I fought alongside became my brothers. I cannot pretend to know what you're feeling now, but I did lose many friends on the battlefield."

"I'm sorry. I'm not so forgetful as to think I'm the only one who has suffered."

Henry looks at me, dropping for once his dapper air, his shield of faded gentility. "The war took more from me than I care to admit. Not just friends, but time." He looks down into his glass, swirling the liquid till it sloshes. "I should be married already, shouldn't I? But it's too late now, I suppose— I've become an old man."

I think of Jane's flushed cheeks out on the lane, and wonder if I misread their meaning. "You're the same age my father was when he met and married my mother. She was much younger, but they were so in love. You must do as he did: Seize the opportunities life puts before you. For happiness—for love."

"Your father gave up much for love, it's true." His tone is still dark, but after a moment he shakes his head slightly, as though driving off sad thoughts, and absently runs a hand down his bad leg—a gesture I've noticed is a habit of his.

"That was your grandfather's favorite chair," he says, in the tone of a man hoping to change the subject. "Uncomfortable enough to make sitting a penance, but very beautifully made."

I've never heard my grandfather characterized in any but glowing terms, and my curiosity is piqued.

"He was never quite at ease with being born into riches," says Henry. "He was, at heart, a self-made man—but one who never got the opportunity to prove it. That is, perhaps, why he liked your Mr. Simpson so much."

"*My* Mr. Simpson?" I say, too flustered to ask what his connection was with my grandfather.

"I saw you two talking outside of the church," says Henry, "and it looked as if you were engaged in some kind of quarrel."

"Certainly not a lovers' quarrel, if that's what you were thinking. Good lord, the man can hardly bear a moment of my company." I feel my cheeks growing pink in the recollection. "He wished to speak immediately of wills and of my responsibilities to the inheritance, mere minutes after my brother was laid to rest. I found it disrespectful."

Henry scowls. "The man has always had cheek, but I did not realize he would be so indelicate. Grace and I are your guardians now, and we will do our best to protect you until you've come of age. But, as you say, these are conversations for another time. For now you must be good to yourself. You'll find everything easier to bear once you've had time to recover from this shock."

I nod slowly, fully aware that he has delicately directed our conversation away from the subject of George's "accident."

When we rejoin the others, we find Grace and Jane playing a listless hand of cards, and Mr. Dowling drowsing with a brandy in front of the fire. Soon Elsie brings in a cold luncheon of meats and preserves. The drink Henry gave me, so bracing at first, now makes me feel hollow and heady. But my nose is still clogged with the scent of dying roses, and I cannot eat a bite.

I bide my time until I can contrive to be alone with Mr. Dowling. I know from the glances the others give me that I look as haunted as I feel, but I cannot rouse myself on their account.

When no opportunity to speak in private with the magistrate arises, I finally stand and stretch. "Mr. Dowling, I wish to have a bit of exercise. Perhaps you would like to accompany me to the library?" Grace looks pleased by this attempt at courtesy, though Henry does not.

As for Mr. Dowling, his eyes light up. "Oh, very good. I'm afraid I did not have nearly enough time with your books on my last visit—such a collection you have here at Walthingham."

The library is on the second floor, close to our living quarters, and its contents are well chosen and well thumbed, unlike the uncut books Grace keeps for show on the first floor. But I can't take comfort in it now that George is gone—it was his favorite place when he wasn't painting.

"May I, Lady Katherine?" says Mr. Dowling. His hands hover hungrily over the nearest shelf.

"First I must speak with you, sir. I confess I pulled you away for my own purposes."

His eyes are kind, though he pats the spines of the books with quick regret. We sit in red leather chairs beneath a severe oil painting of a pale-lipped dowager—one of my ancestors, no doubt. Beneath her disapproving stare, I repeat the fears that I laid out for Henry, but in a calmer, practiced tone. I desperately need him to find me credible, but I needn't have bothered.

"My dear, the sooner we move on from this terrible accident, the better. I see that you do not like that word, but an accident it most assuredly was." He looks down at his hands, clearly regretting what he must say. "Dr. Ebner examined the body, and he is well aware of the wound on your brother's head. It would have been caused by his fleeing horse, or by the stone edging of the bridge. George is buried and at peace, and he would want you to make peace, too."

I can't believe that he won't even consider my words. "Sir, you are a magistrate, and I must respect your opinion on the matter. But I have a sister's heart. How can I make peace, still believing that someone has done this to my brother?"

"I'm a magistrate, but I'm also a man. I've learned that it's best to let the past be the past, lest you find yourself incapable of going on. My beloved wife perished when Jane was just twelve. She was a brilliant woman. Wonderful." He removes his spectacles and presses finger and thumb into the corner of his eyes. "I will tell you honestly, Lady Katherine, that the shock of her passing almost overwhelmed me. Made me question my faith in this world. But I pulled through. I had to, for Jane."

"I'm sorry to make you recount it," I say. "Thank you for your time, sir."

He leaves the library, his shoulders slightly stooped. Yes, he knows of loss, but I still believe he's wrong. Dwelling on the past is the only thing keeping me together. I owe my brother that much, even if no one else can see it.

CHAPTER 9

AFTER JANE AND her father have gone home, after Henry and Grace have urged me into eating a few bites of dinner, after I've washed and undressed, I must face sleep.

Elsie puts me down with a cup of hot milk, nervously plucking at her apron front as I dutifully drink it down. The fuzzy scum of its boiled skin coats my teeth. Under my dressing maid's watch, I slump back into my pillow, feigning readiness for sleep. She turns down the lamp and exits, softly closing the door behind her.

My mind's too dull for thought, too fretful for slumber. I toss in bed until the sheets are hot and twisted, damp against my skin. And when I finally drift away, a nightmare comes, as I knew it would.

I'm in a moving carriage, rattling swiftly down a night-black road. I look ahead—no driver. At first I think I'm alone, until I realize that a dark-haired man is sitting beside me. Without speaking, he takes my hand, then places his mouth on my throat. I shudder with some unnamed emotion as he moves his hands to loosen my dress. I'm wearing my heavy mourning clothes, but they fall away at his touch. Over his shoulder, through half-closed eyes, I see moonlight spilling over the lane ahead of us. The steaming horses are snow white, though it might be a trick of the light.

Then a man stumbles into view. He falls to the ground in front of our carriage, his chest soaked dark with some terrible liquid. It's George, his familiar face twisted with pain. He throws out his hands. His mouth moves silently, calling for us to stop. But I close my eyes, giving in to the man beside me, moving his mouth over mine. Our bodies press in a hot embrace as the carriage wheels shudder over the body of my lost brother.

I wake hot and terrified, fighting against the sheets wound tight around my legs. After a long, panicked moment I remember where I am.

Who was the man beside me? Not John, with his corn-colored hair. The man had dark hair, curling around his collar. I shudder, feeling the ghost of his fingertips on my skin. Could the chilly, distant lawyer have made it into my dreams? More important, does some part of me believe that I am to blame for my brother's death? I close my eyes, remembering the night of the party. George was long abed when the three men threatened Jane and me, and I know that he was at Walthingham in the morning, because he went out painting the day that he died.

I bolt straight up in bed. The painting! George left the

house on his final morning to go paint, but he never came back.

The painting, however, did.

Whoever tucked it back into his room did so to keep us from knowing, a little while longer, that something happened to George. And that person has access to Walthingham Hall.

I think of the hallways and unused corridors, the dusty hive of staircases and servants' quarters and hidden nooks that make up the old estate. A guest from the party could easily have stayed behind; a disgruntled neighbor or former servant could surely slip in. And what of the men I overheard threatening John?

The air in my room is close and sweltering, and I long for the cool of the unheated hallway. Stealing over to my door, I turn the knob.

It sticks. I rattle it, with increasing confusion but no effect. Stella wakes at the noise and joins me, whining and sticking her nose to the bottom seam of the door. When I crouch, peering through the keyhole, it's blocked.

Somebody has locked it from the outside.

I stand, prickling with gooseflesh, and retreat deeper into my room. The door seems suddenly malign, hovering and impassable in the dimness. I know I could call out, beat my palms on the door, but I'm struck with the sudden, vertiginous feeling of distrusting anyone who might hear me.

I go to the window and move the heavy curtain aside, looking out at the oddly bright night. When I close my eyes, I can still see the shape of the tree line imprinted on my eyelids, so vivid is the moonlight reflecting on snow. The forbidding boundary of the woods pulses in my sight, and I stare until my eyes start to blur. Then I blink, and in the same instant I think I see a figure moving, black on black, through the trees. But my head aches from the glare, and I can't be sure. The window frames me, exposing my form to the mysterious scrutiny of that snow-furred strip of trees. Quickly, I climb back into bed, whistling for Stella to join me.

My mind races as I clutch her furry body. Who locked me in? Surely not Elsie, unless she was instructed to do so—perhaps Grace has learned of my recent late-night wanderings. It could be I'm being protected, not from the dangers without, but from myself.

When I wake, the sun is high, and I wince at the light pouring in.

Elsie enters, her head down, carting a ewer full of hot water. My mouth is parched; I wish she'd brought something cool to drink. She still can't look me full in the face without her mouth beginning to tremble, and I find it exhausting—it's work enough managing my own grief.

Listlessly I sit up in bed, feeling as though my limbs have been filled with sand. "Elsie," I say through dry lips, "why was my door locked from the outside last night?"

She keeps her attention on my toilette, her face bland. "It never was, Lady Katherine. Did you try to open it?"

"I did. Perhaps Mrs. Whiting locked it?"

"She couldn't have, Lady Katherine. I'm the one who tends to you; nobody else would have reason to be at your door." She clasps her hands together, nervous. "Could the lock have caught a bit? Perhaps I am to blame. . . ."

"Don't trouble yourself," I say quickly. "It's possible I was mistaken." Was I still lost in a dream when I rattled the knob? I'm not inclined to pursue the question in the light of day.

Elsie still hovers before me, and I'm wearying of her solicitousness. "Please, I can do that myself." I push her hand and its warm washcloth aside, as kindly as I can, not wanting to be touched. "Have Grace and Henry gone down yet?"

"Henry's gone out to walk the paths with John. They want to be sure they're clear for the shoot on Saturday."

A hot confusion takes hold of me. "The shoot?"

"Yes, it's the annual winter shoot. The men come from miles away. . . ." She fades to silence, seeing my face.

"But surely they aren't going ahead with it—my brother is barely in the ground."

"I don't know. Perhaps your cousins thought . . ."

"Never mind," I say in a quieter tone. "I understand you have little to do with these things. Where is my lady cousin, then?"

"She's talking with Mrs. Whiting, arranging for the guests' rooms after the sport is over."

I fall back limply. Is it not a disgrace for Walthingham Hall, a house in mourning, to accept guests? I feel myself unequal to speaking with anyone but Elsie and my own kin— and a dark anger nips at me, that my cousins have selfishly failed to cancel their plans.

Perhaps my maid has read my mind, or maybe my thoughts are written on my exhausted features. She moves to my side and finally looks me full in the face. "I think it's wrong, and . . . and *rotten*," she says quietly, "that they should have a hunt here so soon. They should respect their dead better than that."

She looks fearful already, at her own audaciousness, but I take her hand gratefully. "Thank you. That means more to me than you realize. I think I'd like to be alone for a few hours— why don't you take the morning to visit the stables?"

She turns quickly toward the door, as if to see whether Grace is nearby, as though my cousin could possibly pick up on my meaning. When she turns back to me, her eyes are bright. "Matt and I have never done anything *improper*," she says in a pleading tone. "You'll not tell anyone, my lady?"

"I wouldn't. Is he your beau, then?"

"He's my fiancé," she says, marveling at the exotic word on her tongue. "We'll be married someday, when he's been promoted. Not that we assume a promotion! But we *hope*."

I feel a discrediting prickle of envy, coveting the simple, unbroken state of my dressing maid's hopes. "I would that it happens just as you wish," I say, smiling as best as I can.

CHAPTER 10

As SOON AS Elsie is out of view, I dash from bed, button myself into the simplest of the new-smelling black mourning dresses Grace had made for me, and tiptoe into the hallway. My heart ticks uneasily when I reach for the door-knob, but it opens easily. Stella would most certainly whine if I left her behind, so I let her pad along beside me.

Undetected, I walk to George's chambers. I expect to be flooded with sadness when I open the door, but the room no longer holds any trace of him. It's as flat and indifferent as a stranger's lodgings, filled with the bright new things that he barely touched. Only the painting retains any trace of him, still sitting grimly on its easel in the center of the sitting room. I don't know exactly what I'm looking for here, but when I study the painting afresh, I find it.

There's something within its painted surface that I didn't

see before: in the distance, on the left-hand side, the very edge of Walthingham's walls intrudes into the image. The dried paint feels grainy under my fingertips. I imagine George bending his head to his work, sketching in Walthingham, painting layers of gray over ghostly white branches. Did an approaching shadow fall over his canvas? Did someone call his name? A stranger, or someone he knew, someone he trusted? Using a dull painting knife, I slice the canvas raggedly from its frame.

Downstairs, now wrapped in my heavy cloak, I slip through a side door, clutching the rolled canvas and the painting knife—for protection or for luck, I'm not sure which. I hear the buzz of Grace and the housekeeper making their plans as I exit. "Please clear the flowers away, Mrs. Whiting," says Grace in a tone of light regret. "We needn't ask our guests to dwell on the family's loss."

Her words cut me. The elaborate mourning customs of English society dictate that I wear black for half a year—yet my heart, hidden beneath dark crepe, is expected to be a forgetful thing. I try to forgive Grace, who barely knew my brother, but I feel a grudge nesting its claws into my chest. She is already moving on, and means to move the house with her.

The air outside is silent but for occasional trills of birdsong, and I see neither John nor Henry. It's for the best, as I'm in no mood to keep my opinions to myself. Unfurling the canvas, I try to imagine George's last trek across Walthingham's grounds. I begin to walk counterclockwise around the house, keeping it always to the left of me, as the painting dictates. I give the west wing a wide berth, unwilling to go near its strange topography of uncut stone. An inviting footpath angles into the forest, and I take it on a whim. Low-hanging branches clumped together with ice give the path the appearance of a cool white tunnel.

Sure now that I'm beyond sight of prying eyes, I follow the path into the woods. My dog and I walk in silence, deeper into the trees. Black branches shudder against a nickel-colored sky, and my boots crunch on the ground. The cold is starting to seep through the soles already. Stella frisks at my heels, unbothered by the air; I envy her furry coat.

If I turned left, I'd soon reach the overgrown track once used to carry stone from Walthingham's quarry. To my right, the treacherous half-frozen lake is just visible through the trees. I continue down the path, passing through the sparser woods at the edge of the tree line. When I see in the distance a decrepit lodge hunched between two great oaks, it brings to mind the strange old gamekeeper—McAllister. I'm certain this must once have been his cabin, and I wonder why Henry never hired another to his post. If nothing else, it would serve to deter poachers.

I trudge in my ruined boots deeper into the trees, until the lodge stands between myself and open ground. Its roof slumps with snow and lack of patching, and several window-panes are shattered into sparkling spiderwebs. My skin prickles as the trees overhead encroach on open sky, folding me in with their whip-thin arms. A thaw is coming: The air is fresh with the scent of wet wood, and the air rings with the musical pops and shifts that mark the melting of ice on branches. This chorus was one of George's favorite springtime sounds.

The path stops at the lodge, so from there I trudge along uneven ground, over buried roots and half-submerged stumps.

My breath is smoke on the air. The forest covers several hect-
ares, and after five minutes I look back and realize I can no
longer see the house's wide lawn through the trees. The woods
around me whisper with an icy wind, and a faraway branch
cracks. My breath stops, ragged. Another crack, this one
closer, and Stella speeds off toward the sound.

"Stella!" I cry, but it comes out like a croak.

I take a few steps after her, but she's gone.

"Dammit, Stella," I growl.

I listen for the patter of her paws, but hear nothing.

Then, I feel the unmistakable weight of being watched, of
somebody's eyes on the goose-bumped skin of my exposed
neck. I turn in a slow circle and see nothing but trees.

I tug my coat tighter to my throat. It might just be the cold.

"Stella?" I say again, my voice a near whisper.

A crow caws in response, just behind me, and I nearly
jump out of my cloak. It sits hunched on a low branch, its eyes
black buttons. I wave my hands at it. "Stop watching me, you
awful thing."

The crow flaps lazily through the trees. I walk toward the
place where Stella disappeared, calling her name. When I see
prints in a patch of snow, they look too deep to belong to such
a little dog—perhaps they were left by a fox or a deer; I can't
tell. A voice in my mind, unbidden: *Just torn up, as if in spite.*
"What nonsense," I say aloud, and feel foolish. Then there's a
single, urgent bark, sounding terribly faraway. I yell out to
my dog, but when she barks again, it's muted by snow and
seems to come from no particular direction at all.

The trees look identical, and snow paints the ground an
eerie shade of blue. The sky is flat gray where I can see it

through the trees, and I find no shadows by which to navigate.

Then I feel it again, the eyes on my neck. I hold myself perfectly still, counting to three, and then spin around.

A flash of dark movement, something retreating into the wood some yards away. In my shock I stumble backward, stepping on the hem of my cloak and falling to the ground. My breath catches in my throat as I strain to see through the trees, ignoring the freeze spreading through my backside. I daren't move. There's something there, standing motionless behind a tree. I can sense its shape, rising and falling, rising and falling, with slow, deliberate breaths. Then it shifts again, detaching itself from a trunk and slipping away.

Then I shriek as wet fingers graze my neck . . . until I realize that it's only Stella's cold nose. I let her snuff into my skin another moment, wondering what I just saw. *If* I saw anything at all.

"You're a menace," I mutter to my dog, climbing to my feet and dusting off my cloak.

I press on into the trees, picking up a broken branch to use as a walking stick. And a childish part of me mutters, *just in case I need it*. The woods are dark and I'm beginning to doubt my path when I see a small hill rising out of the trees just ahead, covered in frost-stiffened brambles. I know that George could not resist such a vantage point. When I scramble to the top of it, dropping my makeshift stick in the snow, I see that I'm right. I lift the painting into place before me, and it becomes a surreal window onto bare painted branches, imposed over the snowy landscape. Just as it appears in the painting, only the upper portion of the house is visible, and I realize I've come a considerable distance. I know, with absolute certainty, that I am standing on the place where my brother spent his last hours. Tracing the vast, lonely landscape with my eyes, I say a silent prayer that the white birches were still in his sight when he died.

Stella is sniffing along the ground at my feet; suddenly she goes taut, giving out a low growl that raises goose bumps on my neck. I cast a quick glance into the trees, but she's worrying at the dirty snow.

"What have you found, love?" I whisper. My heart seizes as I spy a paintbrush, half-submerged in muck. I fall to my knees and reach a tentative finger out to touch it. The handle is dotted with clots of dried red.

Growing up on a farm, you instinctively know the look of blood, the close, metallic smell of it. Every animal we ate, my father first bled from the throat, and I've seen animals giving birth more times than I can count. This is not paint or dirt.

I gaze at the terrible proof in my hands and in the snow at my feet, weak with a strange mix of relief and horror. Pain, too, knowing that George must have suffered here, alone and scared.

Stella's growl rises in intensity, and I move to calm her. Then I see the gaunt, dark figure watching me silently from the other side of the rise.

CHAPTER 11

THE OLD POACHER approaches steadily, his strange bright eyes on mine. He carries a crook before him, and I can't tell whether he means it to threaten or to imply that he's harmless. I feel like a fool for tossing my branch aside.

I stand slowly, certain that a sudden move will bring him bearing down on me, crook or no. Stella hides behind my legs, and I decide to be brave on her behalf. "I know who you are, Mr. McAllister. What right do you have to walk on my land?" My voice is shrill in my ears.

He laughs, a hard bark. "Well, well, the little lady of Walthingham. You call this your land, do you?"

I bristle, my fist tight around the paintbrush. "It's mine by law. I *am* the lady of Walthingham Hall, and you'll explain your presence on my grounds at once."

"Or what, you'll set your dog on me?" He laughs again,

his eyes spinning toward Stella in a way that makes me wonder if he's drunk. "It's no good deed you're doing, keeping that runt alive. Poor little thing, she's good for naught but drowning."

The brutal twinkle in his eyes when he says the word "drowning" makes me dizzy. He must know the coroner marked that as George's official cause of death—and now here he is, sniffing around the last place I know George to have been alive. I jab the paintbrush into the air before me. "Perhaps I'm not the only heir of Walthingham Hall to have met you here on this hill. Perhaps you have come back not to dishonor yourself with theft but to hide the proof of what you've done!" My voice shakes, unsure. But McAllister barely seems to hear my words, looking at the brush in my hand with a small frown.

"What are you holding there?"

I move the brush behind my back, defensive. "Did you not hear me? Have you nothing to say for yourself?"

Again he ignores my words. "Is that all you've armed yourself with, out here in these woods? You think there's nothing here that can harm you but the crows?"

"What are you talking about? What do you know about these woods?"

Leaning heavily on his stick, he moves closer. His gait is slow and dragging, and some of the fear goes out of me. "I was gamekeeper here since my own father died, when you weren't even born. It was I who taught your father to fish. I know more of these woods and what they hold than you can imagine. And I know that you're a silly chit meddling in affairs you don't understand." He moves closer to me, and my body goes rigid under the force of his gaze. "You'll be better off going home to your velvets and your balls. This is no place for girls like you."

Stella has edged out from behind me and is sniffing submissively at his feet. He nudges her hard, making her yelp. "Or for a *beast* like this."

He turns and begins limping away as I scoop Stella into my arms.

"Wait!" I cry. "I want to talk to you!"

He looks back once, his eyes sharp on mine, then slips through a break in the trees.

After standing a moment in the chill sunlight on the rise, I roll the canvas and stuff it inside my coat, then scoop up Stella and set a brisk pace down the hill, following my own tracks. I hug Stella so tightly to my chest that she lets out a strangled whimper, but I can't seem to loosen my grip. Foolishly, I fear that the opening in the trees will never come, that I will be lost again in these malevolent woods. But the ground soon clears, and sunlight sifts through a thinning cover of branches. The wind carries the crackling scent of fire, and I see a smoke trail curling over the trees—John and Henry must be burning brush. I'm angry afresh at this reminder of the hunt.

When I step back out onto Walthingham's lawn, hunched miserably over the paintbrush and my poor dog, the two men are standing between the house and me. Their heads are tucked close into their chests, and they haven't yet noticed my arrival. Lingering at the edge of the woods, I can see the dark look on Henry's face; John's is turned away from me. I stop short when Henry stabs a finger into the footman's broad chest, speaking fierce words I cannot hear. At last he throws up his hands, turns heel, and stalks off toward the front of the house. I wonder if John is speaking on my behalf, against the hunt, but realize that no footman would dare contradict the wishes of the house in that way. John, then, must have done something wrong.

I think I'll wait until he's disappeared to walk across open ground, but Stella wriggles in my arms and lets out a yap. John turns sharply, then, spying me, rushes toward us.

He won't meet my eyes as he pulls off his coat and wraps it around my shoulders, atop my own heavy cloak. "Lady Katherine, you should not be walking these woods. The cold alone is dangerous."

"Please," I protest. "I'm warm enough without it, and you'll freeze."

"No, you're shivering," he says, his expression lightening. "I won't have you carried off by a chill before I've got my reading lessons in."

Ducking my head, I allow him to mistake my state of misery for a chill, and for a moment neither of us speaks. My hands are warm beneath my cloak, clutching the paintbrush safely to my chest, but something stops me from telling him what I've found. Instead I gesture toward Henry's retreating back. "You were discussing something with my cousin. I hope nothing is wrong?"

He makes a dismissive gesture. "I don't think this shoot should take place," he says. For a moment my heart leaps, but he continues. "The grounds are unsafe after the snowfall—and the weather is warming; soon it will be nothing but slush."

If he catches my disappointed look, he does not say. "I

should not keep you out here in conversation. I think the doctor would prefer you be abed."

"I would be, but my dog ran off, and I was bound to follow."

"Not much of a lady, that one," he says. "Or so I've been told."

I can't meet his keen, smiling eyes. Firmly I return his coat, still keeping one hand out of view. "I'm not very cold anymore, truly. I'll go inside to warm up."

Then I imagine Grace and Mrs. Whiting, buzzing about the house making plans, clearing away every sign that ours was ever a house in mourning, and think again. "Perhaps you can help me, John—do you think you can get me into my rooms unseen? My cousins will worry if they knew I was following after Stella again."

He touches two fingers to his head in mock salute. "As you wish, Lady Katherine. I daresay I know the secret ways of Walthingham better than any American girl."

Before I can decide whether that's more cheek than I should allow, he's started away, and I have no choice but to follow.

It isn't until we're creeping up the servants' stairs that I realize the canvas is no longer tucked inside my cloak. I must have dropped it somewhere in the woods. For a moment I consider rushing back out to find it. But with John at my side and Grace prowling about below, I know that I can't. My freedom here is curtailed. I curse myself for losing one-half of my evidence—and the last painting that George will ever make.

CHAPTER 12

I SPLASH MY FACE with water, cooled in the basin and fresh on my skin. My eyes in the glass are unnaturally bright. But it doesn't matter anymore what my cousins think of my temper—I have proof that my brother was murdered, and finally they must listen.

I slip off my waterlogged boots and set them before the fireplace, then step into the black pair I wore to yesterday's funeral. My fingers are cold and stiff, fumbling with the tiny patent buttons. Around me the house bustles with the same sparkling energy that preceded the ball, as if nothing's changed between that night and this. Clutching the paintbrush in my hands, chapped from hours spent traipsing through the woods, I imagine their faces when I finally show them. Realization, followed by slow horror. A messenger will be dispatched to the magistrate, and McAllister will be dragged in for questioning.

I find Grace in an alcove near to the servants' quarters, interrogating a tiny redheaded serving boy. She takes one look at my avid, windburned face and dismisses him. He throws me a look of gratitude and scampers away.

"Katherine, good Lord," Grace says nervously. "You look a fright—please tell me you haven't been out in this bad weather."

"Grace," I say.

"Oh, my dear," she presses on. "Look at your poor hands!" My hands were almost delicate after three weeks under her tutelage, but now they're red and scored with scratches. "Did your mutt do this?"

"Grace," I say again, more loudly. "Let me speak. The hunt cannot go on—you and Henry must call it off immediately."

She looks at me blankly for a moment, then with dawning embarrassment. "Oh, I see," she says faintly. "I understand the timing seems a bit . . . Certainly we are heartbroken about George, but this hunt is annual, and planned very far in advance. Many have come from quite far, and—Oh!"

She gasps a bit as I hold out the paintbrush. "What is this?" she asks with puckered distaste.

"My brother's paintbrush, Grace. I went to the hill where he was painting just before he was killed—*killed*, Grace. And this paintbrush was there, on the ground, and you can see that it's covered with blood. There was blood in the snow, George's blood, and now you must, you *must* see that my brother's death was not an accident."

I say this with a kind of desperate triumph, but her face does not change. After a silent moment inspecting my face, then the brush, then back again, she says, "Blood, Katherine, or paint?"

"Good God, Grace! Are you not hearing me? I found this in the very spot where my brother was at work before he died—is this not worth investigating, at the very least?"

A step in the hallway, and Henry rounds the corner, his face concerned. "Katherine, why are you raising your voice? Has something happened?"

"Yes, something has happened. My brother has been killed, and I'm very close to proving it!" With a shaking hand, I place the paintbrush carefully on a small side table. Henry leans forward from the waist to inspect it; when he gets close enough to see the blood, his face blanches.

"What is this, Katherine? Where did you get it?"

"This is my brother's blood, on his paintbrush. I found the place where he was painting just before he died, and this was buried in the snow. Stella found it, really. And the old poacher, Mr. McAllister, came upon me there—what are the chances that he would be at the very spot? He knows something, Henry—something he doesn't want to say."

Henry's voice is low, angry, but perfectly controlled, and I have a flash of how he must have been on the battlefield. "That man has been wandering the estate unheeded long enough. Your grandfather always showed him leniency, but I'm through following his example. What exactly did he say to you?"

"He didn't say much—but he's dangerous, I'm sure of it. Please, come with me into the woods, and we can find the spot again. We must send for Mr. Dowling and show him what I've found!"

"Katherine, you look terrible." Grace says this with unexpected steel in her voice. "It is up to me to preserve the health of the last remaining Randolph, and I am going to do so whether you will respect me or not."

I want to cry with frustration. "The cold is broken, and the snow will melt! If we don't look now, the blood will be gone."

She waves my words aside. "It's only the blood of a rabbit, or some other wild thing. Your brother drowned, Katherine. You mustn't drive yourself mad."

"It's very likely that McAllister killed one of our animals there," says Henry furiously. "If the man doesn't end up in leg irons, it won't be for my lack of trying."

"No, no," I say. "It was the very spot—the very spot where George stood! I used the painting to find the way!"

Grace and Henry exchange an uneasy look; I realize I sound hysterical. "What painting?" Henry says doubtfully.

"I lost it on the way back; it fell from my cloak." I spin toward the door so fast my head aches. "But I can prove it to you," I cry, speeding out of the room. "Come with me!"

My cousins quickly flank me, Grace glancing nervously behind. When Henry tries to catch my arm, I brush him off. I lead them up the grand staircase, then race toward George's room. When I catch a glimpse of myself in a hallway mirror my face is a ghostly oval, my eyes etched with shadows. I kick at the muddy hem of my dress with every step.

With grim certainty I throw open the door to George's sitting room.

The easel stands in the center of the room, as ever. But the empty frame is gone. I stare at the space where it stood just hours ago. Pressing my palms to my eyes, I feel as if I'm falling.

"Perhaps your brother sent the painting on to London before his accident," Grace says, breathing hard and pressing a hand into her side. She speaks gently, as though loud noises will make me snap.

"Can't you see?" I say wildly. "Someone has done this. Someone is doing this to me."

"Keep your voice down," Grace whispers sharply as two servants carrying rolled bedding pass the door.

Henry places a careful hand on my shoulder, and I twist away. Then a fit of coughing overtakes me, rising with unexpected force from deep within my chest. On its heels I feel a wave of bone-deep weariness.

"I'll have someone bring you something hot to drink," Grace says with renewed vigor, back on terms she understands. "I'll do so right away."

Nobody believes me. Even with proof in my hand, my cousins push my concerns aside. I feel like I'm screaming in a crowded room, and nobody even notices. Henry places a hand on my arm and gently guides me back to my own chambers. When I'm sitting, he squats awkwardly in front of the fire with a bellows, bringing the flames back up to warm me. "I will go to the spot, Katherine," he says, his back still to me. "Just describe the place, and I will find it. If I see anything worrying, I'll get the magistrate's opinion on the matter."

"Thank you," I say dully. I know nothing will come of his promise. He's just as fearful as Grace, just as unwilling to accept that something so terrible could happen at Walthingham Hall.

The faint patter of melting snow outside my window makes

my skin crawl. With every drop I envision the evidence melting away into mud. I realize I left the paintbrush on the table downstairs, but it hardly seems to matter now. I know that it will be gone when I return, spirited away by a servant who will take the stains on the handle for paint.

Elsie comes in carrying a tray of toast and a hot milk posset. Though she *tsks* at me to let it cool, I take hot gulps, welcoming the sear of heat in my chest. Henry stands aside while she serves me, inspecting the combs and effects arrayed on my dressing table with polite indifference. Even though he shares a home with Grace, he's an old bachelor, and a soldier to boot—he seems unused to being around a woman's things.

Finally, Elsie retreats, but Henry stays on. "Bucked up, Katherine?" he says with strained heartiness, his concerned eyes trained on mine. When I don't answer, he takes a seat beside me.

"I don't know where McAllister is staying these days—the old lodge must be too drafty now for even an old hound like him to squat in." He holds his hands to the fire, his face stony. "But I'll catch him out. He won't threaten you again. And he won't humiliate me, not with the shoot about to begin."

"Henry, please." My voice sounds faraway, and I wonder if Elsie put some drowsy-making herb in my milk. "Don't talk to me of hunting now—how can you even think of it? How can it not be a disgrace to our house, to forget my brother so soon?"

The face he turns toward me is contrite. "I understand you must think us cold, Katherine. Your loss comes so quickly on the heels of mine—of ours. My uncle, your grandfather: He raised me after my own father died." His face twists a moment, like he's tasted something bitter. "My father was dissolute, a drinker, but your grandfather taught me how to be a man. A *public* man. Our lives are not entirely our own, living on display as we do. We must lose ourselves in routine, and so lose our grief. And if we give our neighbors less reason to gossip, so much the better."

"Is the hunt so important?" I ask wearily.

He shrugs slightly, staring at the fire. "Not the hunt, but what it stands for. For Walthingham Hall and its decades of tradition. For strength in the face of terrible adversity. For soldiering on when you want only to give up."

I'm tired, too tired to argue. I let my head drop back onto my chair. "I understand, Henry. Just, please, let me sleep now."

As he stands and softly exits the room, I'm already drifting away.

The light when I wake slants low through the windows. My head is still fuzzy, but I finally feel as if I could eat. Under a covered tray on the table near the fire I find two hard-cooked eggs, a roll, still warm, and stewed rabbit in dark gravy. My stomach turns at the sight of the meat, but I keep the rest of it down.

With one hand to my aching head, I write a note to Jane, asking her to come see me before the shoot. I would feel guilty, asking her again to tend to me in my mourning, but I know she'll welcome the chance to see Henry.

Soon Grace comes in, and I see her relief that my wild mood has calmed into mere wretchedness. She reads over the note before folding it and sending it off with a footman; I know its mundane contents must comfort her.

While she does so, I move to the window to gaze out onto the grounds. Twilight hovers like purple haze over the tree line. The snow has all but melted away.

CHAPTER 13

Elsie looks at me, unsure. "Bring this note to John, Lady Katherine? To footman John?"

I watch her blandly, making my face as blank as paper. "Yes, Elsie. Please deliver it to him at once."

She's too perplexed walking out to remember to curtsy, though she dashes back round the corner a moment later to bob a quick one.

My note is simple:

If you're ready for your first lesson, meet me at the entrance to the servants' quarters in an hour.

If I have to lie in bed any longer, to think and cry and wonder, I'll go insane. I can, at least, discharge my promise to John. And I *want* to see him, though I'm scarcely willing to admit it to myself.

Before our appointed meeting time, I dawdle through the

house, touching the shining surfaces of things and wondering at its all being mine. Before George's death, it was easier to think of it as *ours*—indeed, as his and his future wife's. Now it's near impossible to believe I am the sole owner of Walthingham Hall and all its holdings.

George and I had made plans in hushed voices the night after we arrived, tired beyond reason but too excited to sleep. When we docked in Bristol we saw, among the richly arrayed parties of London-bound travelers, scenes of terrible poverty. Worst were the children, malnourished and filthy, tugging at our clothes in the hopes of handouts. Grace had looked straight ahead, clutching her rich coat; Henry had patted one small girl awkwardly on the head when she would not make way for him. George, though, had emptied his pockets, giving them coins and candies. His eyes were damp when we boarded our carriage, and their great need was still on his mind when we arrived at Walthingham.

Now I inspect the family silver, largely unused but kept at a high shine; the books standing in jewel-colored rows, unread. If I was the one lost, and George left behind, what would he do? Would he sell all the contents of Walthingham, gift them to the destitute? Could he still bear to paint after losing me, to have his show at the Academy?

I hear a clock chiming the hour from far away, and it brings a flush to my cheeks. I hurry to find John, half hoping he won't be there.

He is. His shirt, worn thin with starching, is so clean and white that I wonder if he changed it before meeting with me. He doesn't speak for a moment, looking down at his shoes.

"Is there a quiet room we might sit in?" I ask. "Where we won't be disturbed?"

"Perhaps the boot room, my lady? There's a bit of space to sit, and we can carry in a candle."

"Yes, that's perfect," I say, my voice sounding terribly formal in my nervousness. "I'll wait for you here, while you fetch a light."

He nods and strides quickly around the corner. I have time only to contemplate the broadness of his back under pliant white cotton before he's returning, slightly out of breath, a lantern in hand.

Our classroom is close with the smell of polish and shining leather, and an underlying tang of damp earth. John peels back the oilcloth covering a small table, and we sit on footstools, pulled close together within the ring of lantern light.

I empty the contents of my pockets onto the table: ink and paper, a quill and a small book. "Let's start with the letters of the alphabet," I say brightly. "You can show me what you know, and I can fill in the gaps."

He nods and leans his whole body over the page, his brow heavy with concentration. The pen sits clumsily in his hands, staining his fingers with ink, and the letters he forms are marred thickly with blots.

I'm watching the page, nodding, when he drops the pen in disgust. "That's about the length of it, Lady Katherine."

"Don't be frustrated," I say. "Our lesson has just begun."

He leans far back on his stool and pinches the bridge of his nose, leaving smudges on either side. "Might we talk a minute instead? It's close work, glaring at the paper like that. I don't envy those who make their life around it."

I seize the opportunity. "Yes, let's talk. Yesterday, before I met you, I saw old McAllister—the poacher. We . . . didn't speak, I just saw him from afar. Perhaps you can tell me what you know about him."

John watches me warily. "You ought to steer clear of the old man. He frightened me as a child, and if I were honest I'd admit that he frightens me even now."

"But why?" I say. "What was he like?"

"Much like he is now, I suppose. But back then he had the trust of Lord Randolph. He was stern and strict, even cruel. At least, it looked like cruelty to a young boy. I remember one time . . ." He trails off, looking at his hands.

"Tell me," I prompt him.

"Well . . . it might sound a small thing to you. When I was a child I found an injured fox kit, a little thing with red fur and nice tufts to her ears. Her leg was broken, and she should have bitten me when I found her, but she didn't. She could tell I was going to help her."

His voice has gone tender in the telling, his eyes soft. "I brought her to McAllister, asked him to help me make her a splint, to tell me what she might like best to eat. McAllister, the old bastard—pardon me, lady, I should not have said that. But you see, he smothered her. Quickly, with his hand in its old leather glove. She kicked her feet and turned her eyes on me, but I was frozen on the spot. I couldn't do anything but cry—only later, though, once I'd run away. While he was killing her, I just stood there. 'Her leg wasn't going to set right,' he told me. 'She'd never be able to hunt for herself again.' Perhaps he was right. But after that, I never went near him if I could help it. I couldn't bear to look at those mean black gloves he wore."

I've never heard John speak so much in one go, and my heart aches for the child he was. "Whether he was right or not, he needn't have killed something you asked him to protect, as you looked on. That was unkind." The story's shaken me, though more than once I'd seen my own father—even George—putting down an animal that had come to the end of its usefulness. I'd cried my own share of tears over those necessary deaths. Once again, I'm reminded of how much more I have in common with the likes of John and Elsie than with my own cousins.

I'm about to say so when John speaks. "Perhaps we can start our lesson again, Lady Randolph?"

I pull the paper toward me and write my name neatly across it, below his jumble of soupy letters. "Here, this is my name. Will you write your own below it?"

He does so, with relative facility. "That's one I can do," he says. "Before my mother passed, she worked my letters with me a bit. But not any more than a man of my station would need—my father saw to that."

"Let's start with simple words, then, and we'll see what you remember." I turn to the small book of Bible verses, opening it flat on the table. Over the next hour John copies them out under my watchful eye:

No one can serve two masters.
Man is born to trouble, as the sparks fly upward.

The Lord knows the way of the righteous,
but the way of the wicked will perish.
Do not be afraid, for I am with you.

"Do you remember what you asked me that day?" I say quietly. "At the funeral, I mean."

"I think I do."

"You asked whether the dead really watch over us, whether they can be with us still. And I think that my answer is no. Not in any real way. Not in any way that can possibly matter. My mother, my father, my brother—they're all dead. And I am alone."

John places his warm, inky hand over mine as my vision blurs with tears. "I feel like the truth is slipping away from me," I whisper. "About my brother's death. I feel I'm going mad . . . like I'm completely alone, where no one can touch me, or believe me when I say that something about his death is terribly wrong."

I'm crying now, and John pushes the whole heavy table away with one quick motion; in another, he's caught me up into his arms. He smells of soap and smoke and horses—he smells of my life in Virginia. Our faces are suddenly close together, and we grow still, looking at each other as if across some great divide. Then he pushes forward and across, and I lean forward to meet him, and we're kissing, his mouth soft, insistent, our bodies pressed as close as we can make them. He picks me up with ease and places me on the table, and by some instinct I wrap my legs tight around his hips. My mind is racing, racing, my scattered thoughts trying to pull themselves back together, but I can't heed them. I think only of my mouth on his, his hands on my face, on my neck, then under me, supporting me, as he moves his mouth down over my throat. My body feels like one great heartbeat, a pulse of longing; I whisper something, but he doesn't hear. "We shouldn't be doing this" is what I say, but I say it not wanting him to hear. I hook one hand into his pale hair, pulling his mouth back to mine, then reach a hand back to steady myself— and knock over the inkpot, sending black ink swirling over the uncovered table.

John curses, untangling himself from me, as my dress soaks up some of the damage. I can't meet his eyes, until the sound of Mr. Carrick through the door shocks us both upright. "What's going on in there?" he calls in his arrogant voice. "Who's that making such a racket?"

John moves silently to a rack of boots behind us, pulling it out from the wall to reveal the unused door just behind. "I'll take care of Carrick," he says grimly. "You go left out of here. The corridor will turn a few times, but you'll find yourself soon enough."

"No," I say. "You go. Mr. Carrick can't send me running in my own house. I'll be in far less trouble with him than you will."

He considers this for a moment, then nods. "Thank you for the lesson, lady," he whispers as he slips through the door.

When he's gone, I stand dumbly a moment, staring at the space where he was. Then I smooth down my hair, ball up the practice paper in my hand, and unlatch the door for Mr. Carrick.

"What in the world . . ." he says, surveying the ink-stained table, the disarrayed boots, and me. His eyes catch on the two stools, pushed close together by the table. Slowly he brings his gaze to mine, his eyes cool with understanding.

"I was looking for a flint box," I say carelessly. "The fire went out in my room, and you were not close by to light it."

He draws himself up a bit at the cheek in my voice. "I'll send your girl up directly, Miss Katherine. And I'll have a maid see to the mess here."

"Please do so, Carrick. And going forward, I must ask that you call me Lady Randolph. I am, after all, the mistress of Walthingham Hall."

His jaw visibly tightens as he absorbs these words. "Absolutely correct, Lady Randolph," he says. "I will not forget your preferred address again."

When he's gone, I let my body sag with relief against the table—and savor for one slow moment the memory of John's lips, his body on mine. Then I slip the writing paper and verse book back into my pocket and extinguish the candle, leaving it on the table for John to find. My whole body feels heavy as I take the stairs, but more with languor now than grief. Again and again I tell myself that what happened with John cannot be repeated—but the moment I close my eyes, the scent and feel of him floods the darkness behind my lids, so powerfully I can hardly keep my feet.

It's a shock coming face-to-face with my lady cousin at the second-floor landing.

"Katherine! I won't ask why you're not in bed—it seems we can't keep you there longer than a moment. But why on earth are you coming up the servants' stairs?" Her eyes narrow, and I remember the way she looked at me in the churchyard after I spoke to John.

Aware of the red flush on my cheeks, the ink on my dress, I keep my back toward the wall and speak quickly. "I was ashamed of my behavior earlier, Grace. I did not want anyone to see me. I allowed myself to become hysterical, and it was unbecoming."

Her face relaxes. "You've been through so much," she says soothingly. "I've put a glass of medicine by your bed, and you must take it straightaway—Dr. Ebner gave it to me, in the case of any emotional outbursts."

Her words make me want to fling the glass against a wall, but I make myself smile. "Thank you for your thoughtfulness, Grace. Perhaps it will help me sleep, at last."

I keep a small smile on my face as she goes, her obvious suspicion not quite spent. When she's out of sight, I race to my rooms, holding my inky skirts in my hands. I strip to my underclothes to inspect them, and see that the ink has merely stiffened my mourning clothes without changing their color. Nevertheless, I hide the dress in the very back of my closet, thinking that I will ask Elsie to help me with it in a week or two, when any word of the mysterious ink spill, spread by Mr. Carrick, has passed from the other servants' minds.

I lock my door from the inside and sniff at the medicine Grace left for me. I'd had no intention of taking it, but it looks and smells very like a hot milk posset, so I swallow it down.

My thoughts as I lie back on my bed are, for once, not of George alone. With a secretive feeling that's a sister to guilt, I try to imagine myself living with John in a humble cottage. In my mind's eye, it's much like the gamekeeper's cottage, but patched up and shining. Then I turn restlessly in bed, punch my pillow down, and see John living with me here at

Walthingham Hall. Wearing the clothes of a lord, ordering our dinner from Mr. Carrick . . .

Neither vision will hold for long, so I fall asleep imagining the two of us in Virginia, walking hand in hand over the acres of my lost family farm. Finally, my drifting thoughts spin into dreams, none of which I can remember.

When I wake hours later, I'm stiff and lying in utter blackness. The fire has burned to nothing, and the air is cold. But I sit upright fast, my heart racing, because there is someone with me in the room. The steady sound of breathing fills my ears, just perceptible beneath the wind tapping around my windows.

There—in the corner—something crouches. A dark shape, too hunched to be a man. As I adjust to the blackness, my sight sharpens, and I see two yellow eyes watching me. My breath stops in my throat. *This can't be happening.* Keeping my eyes on the thing, I move my legs to the floor, carefully, carefully. It keeps its terrible gaze trained back on mine.

My hands fumble over the bedside table until they find the lamp. Working quietly, my heart loud in my ears, I struggle to light it with clumsy fingers. The thing shifts in the gloom, and I *feel* a low growl stirring the hair on my neck.

Then the lamp catches, the room fills with flickering light, and the terrible, crouching creature becomes my fainting couch, over which is folded a winter cloak, ordered before George's death and newly arrived. The amber brooch pinned at its neck is an outstretched butterfly, its wings painted with twin gold circles that glimmer with reflected moonlight.

I lie down once more, but I leave the lamp burning.

CHAPTER 14

THE BAYING OF Henry's hounds breaks the fragile quiet of the morning. Standing next to Grace on the terrace, I feel as brittle in the sunlight as if I were made of blown glass. Stella rolls in the frozen grass below me, her nose loving the flood of smells brought with the men and their hounds and horses. The lawn unfurls from our feet to the tree line, where the riders cluster around my cousin. He sits proud on his mount, the not-so-young gentleman of Walthingham Hall. I've never seen him look so fresh and fine—it's a shame Jane isn't here beside me. Though her father sits in the honored place next to Henry, his daughter did not join him. I realize I'm very poor company at present, but am hurt that she did not at least respond to my note.

At a gesture from Henry, Grace leads me down onto the

lawn to bid them a good hunt. But for John and Matt, serving as grooms, the men are all Henry's age or older. Because of the angle of the sun behind him, I can't make out John's face. I take care not to look at him too long.

"I hope you shoot many birds, brother," says Grace. "Though I do find it distasteful myself. Bloodshed is not known to bring out the good in people."

A man with a black mustache, seated on a great bay stallion, clicks his tongue smartly. "Shooting is a man's occupation! A gentlewoman like you need not trouble herself about it."

Grace foolishly dips her head, but my blood goes hot. For a moment I am the Katherine of a year ago. "It's not so much trouble for *all* women," I say, and in one quick movement pull a rifle from the sling that Matt carries. Turning toward a great bank of ornamental hedges, I catch the silliest one in my sights. It's shaped like a cockerel, and in one clean blast I shave off its comb.

A thick spray of greenery falls at the foot of the shrubbery, and gray smoke dissipates into the blue. "Thank you for the use of this," I say, handing the gun back to poor Matt. I ignore the censure in Grace's eyes—her mouth is tucked so tight she looks lipless. For a moment the gentlemen simply gape at me, until Henry slaps his thigh and begins to laugh. "Very good show, cousin—you've gelded the gardener's cockerel! I must ask him his thoughts on the new hen of Walthingham."

The other men join in his laughter; only Grace continues to look embarrassed. But my rush of pride soon subsides, leaving me feeling hollow. My brother should be here, astride

Croxley. He was a better hunter than any of these men are likely to be. *And wouldn't they feel foolish when the artist bested them all at their sport.* George never had to prove himself to be a good man, he simply was one. Fighting back a tide of directionless anger, I turn sharply and begin walking toward the house. At my back, a hunting horn sounds, signaling the departure of the men and their retinue.

I turn around once and see John gazing straight back at me. His smile is fathomless and puts a quiver into my knees. *Steel in your spine, girl.* Quickly, I walk on, until a call from behind slows my pace.

Grace huffs toward me in her purple cloak. "Katherine, that was not in entirely good taste." The look or the shooting? I shrug my agreement, thinking of the empty hours ahead. Today, I decide, I must write the painful letter I have long delayed, informing my foster family of George's death. That will be the end of it—no more thinking I can dream it away. The surreal horror of his being gone will become real.

". . . you must, of course, sit in on the interview, as she'll be tending to you." Grace has been speaking as I daydreamed, and I'm pulled back quickly to the present.

"I'm sorry, Grace. To whom are you referring? What interview?"

"For your new lady's maid, of course. A young woman will be here at eleven, and we will be discussing her qualifications in the lesser parlor."

"But why? Elsie does her work ably, and I like her. Grace, I do not need a second maid."

"Good lord, girl, your head really is a million miles away.

As I was saying, Elsie must be let go. Mrs. Whiting's orders, and you know I'd trust that woman with anything, even the best of my summer silks. But that's neither here nor there. . . ."

"Let go," I say faintly. "But to where? Walthingham is her home, Grace. And Mrs. Whiting can't let anyone go without my leave."

Grace pulls herself up a bit. "You are the lady of Walthingham, yes, but Mrs. Whiting is in charge of staffing. And she's learned that Elsie has become involved with a young man in the stables—the very one who lent his rifle to your little display. Of course, he'll be on his way, too, directly after the hunt. It's just a shame we needed him for one more day."

I think of Elsie's high hopes, her recent engagement. Taking in my expression, Grace purses her lips. "Don't be so appalled, dear; it's only natural among their sort. Elsie's sister was sent away for just such a thing—the girl had got a child with one of our staff, and we were kind enough to let Elsie stay on without her. That was a foolish mistake we'll be righting today—I should have known such weakness would be a family trait."

So that's where poor Elsie's remaining family has gone. I wonder if they've even told her the truth about it. "But I like Elsie, very much," I say, my voice pleading. "Grace, she's a young girl in love. What foolish things have not been done for love?"

"With that attitude, Katherine, how will you make the proper choices for the running of Walthingham Hall? Many young girls would give much and more for a position here—girls with conduct more fitting to serve our esteemed house."

Her words fall heavy on my ears. "But she's so young, and already she's lost the closeness of a sister to such a mistake. If you'll only let me talk to her, I'm certain I can convince her to break it off with him." I'm not so sure, but I can't see another way of convincing my cousin.

She wavers a moment, then sighs. "Very well. I still think you're being far too generous, but perhaps the girl can stay on without her young man. We cannot foster such a relationship under our roof, so one of them must go. I will consult with Mrs. Whiting—on this one occasion, at the request of Lady Randolph, I think we might give Elsie a final opportunity to prove herself."

She stops altogether then, and turns toward me on the sloping grass. "But you must understand that here, among our kind of people, a young woman's reputation is her most important possession. And you must look to your *own* self, too, and be careful about the amount of time you are spending with a certain young man, a man who may not be employed here much longer if this persists. It has not gone unnoticed, and it is not seemly."

I keep my head high while silently cursing my carelessness—I should have known the flirtation would not pass without consequence. Did she glean our connection from what she saw outside of the church? Or is Mr. Carrick to blame for her suspicions? I press my lips together in shame, then force a smile. "I don't condone gossip, Grace, and I believe you have been given bad information. I haven't been spending time with anyone but Stella. I suppose there are men here who are a good deal handsomer than her, but certainly less playful."

At first she doesn't respond, and I think she'll drop the subject. Then, in a cool tone, she speaks. "I wish you wouldn't take me for such a fool, Katherine—I only look out for your best interests. And though it was never proven, it may interest you to know that the baby Elsie's sister carried was believed by many of the servants to be John's."

With that, she sweeps ahead of me into the house. I stare after her with a sudden sense of foreboding, chilled by more than the wind. A vision of John lying in the hay with another girl—a prettier, older version of Elsie—fills my mind. Is it possible he didn't know she was pregnant? *No*, I think, *he would have known*. If what Grace says is true, he would simply have chosen not to go after her.

I dawdle a moment outside, letting the air cool my cheeks, before I feel equal to taking tea with Grace. When I enter the parlor, she's sitting with perfect equanimity on a sofa. Kneeling before her, eyes downcast and rimmed with red, Elsie arranges a cup of tea from a tray. I marvel at how unmoved Grace is by the girl's plight. She must truly believe that the servants aren't capable of feeling or of grieving the way that her own class can. I wonder, darkly, whether this prejudice has guided her treatment of me in the wake of George's death. Perhaps I will always be a peasant in her eyes, just one that has been more or less trained into placidity.

Mrs. Whiting herself enters soon after. Elsie scurries backward out of the room, barely daring to stand before the older servant's snobbish gaze. Grace draws Mrs. Whiting into a private conference, no doubt relaying my wishes with regards to Elsie, and I quietly follow my dressing maid into the hall.

She's standing in place, shoulders slumped. I touch her elbow gently. "Elsie, it's all right. I spoke to Grace: You won't be let go. I want you working here still, and it's my house, not Mrs. Whiting's. And not Grace's, either."

She's started crying so hard she can't speak for a moment but can only shake her head fiercely. "It's not—it's not that. I don't care what happens to me! It's what will happen to Matt, and that it's all my fault!" She breaks into a fresh round of tears, face buried in her apron. I draw her into an embrace, and her raw unhappiness gives me leave to dwell a moment on my own.

With a final, shuddering breath, Elsie comes back to herself. "I'm not ungrateful," she says immediately. "Thank you, Lady Katherine, for helping me keep my position!"

"Of course. Now go splash your face. We have plenty of tea already, and Mrs. Whiting needn't know you've been crying."

She nods and darts away, hands still twisted into her damp apron.

"Lady *Randolph*."

I spin round to find Mr. Carrick in the hall behind me, looking ill at ease in my presence. I decide this is preferable to his usual air of smug superiority.

"Yes, Mr. Carrick?"

"You have a visitor. Would you like to receive in the morning room or the main parlor?"

I smile, relieved—Jane hadn't ignored my letter after all. "The morning room will do. Please have tea sent in." Our conversation will be more private there.

I settle myself on a pink-and-green-striped sofa, a rare object in this house in that it's both beautiful *and* comfortable. At the soft sound of someone clearing their throat, I look up.

William Simpson is standing in the doorway. Despite his expression, one of soft diffidence, my mind goes instantly to my dream. The ghost of his mouth on my skin, my brother's body in the road. It was him in the dream; now I'm sure of it.

"Lady Katherine?" He holds his hat to his chest, and a leather satchel hangs from his hand.

It takes me a couple of seconds to realize that he is the visitor I am receiving, not my friend. "Yes! Mr. Simpson, I'm sorry. I had a . . . a moment of dizziness. Please sit down."

He takes a seat in a chair just opposite the portrait of my grandfather. I watch his eyes tracing the painted figure. "We met in this room, did we not, Lady Katherine?" His voice has a hint of a smile in it.

The appearance of a maid bearing our tea on a tray saves me from answering. I thank her, then send her away, ducking my head over our cups while waiting for my blush to fade.

"You're here, I suppose, to begin putting the estate's affairs in order?"

It's his turn to redden, shifting with embarrassment in his seat. "We can talk about that if you wish. If you're ready. I'm here only to tell you . . . I don't know what it will mean to you now, but the Royal Academy will be going on with its exhibition of your brother's work. I have corresponded with the curator, and he offers his condolences. He believes the paintings will go for more, even, than they would for a . . ." He looks uncomfortable again. "For a living artist. But I told him I did not think you were willing to sell."

I look at him, surprised by the insight. "Thank you. I would not sell my brother's work to any private houses. But if a museum wished to purchase a painting, I would consider the sale." I speak carefully, and realize that I'd already decided this in my mind, without conscious thought. The idea of my brother's work hanging in a museum, alongside that of the great masters, still sends a sad thrill through me.

Mr. Simpson nods. "Yes, I think that is exactly how I should handle it, were I in your place."

The first distant volley of gunshots echoes through the room, and a furrow appears between his brows. "Have they gone on with the winter hunt, then? So soon after your family's loss?" He looks as if he might say more, but falls silent.

His words are impertinent but echo my own sentiments. "And with my blessing, though I'll admit it was not freely given. Nor was it asked for, until the guests were nearly arrived." My voice sounds bitter to my own ears, so I attempt, feebly, to change course. "Do you often shoot, sir?"

"The pursuit has never interested me. I'm a great walker, but I'd much prefer to carry an umbrella through the streets of London than a gun through the woods. Perhaps that sounds odd to a farm girl, but I suppose my upbringing can be blamed for it."

Something in the way that he says "farm girl" makes me think that he sees my former life as a point of interest, not a weakness. Mr. Simpson swirls the contents of his teacup as shots resound from the woods beyond.

"We can speak on the subject of my will," I say abruptly. "I do wish to have that, at least, under control."

He puts down his cup and pulls paper and a writing utensil from his satchel with practiced swiftness. Giving me an encouraging nod, he leans over a page. That stubborn lock of dark hair falls over his brow, but he pays it no heed.

"I would like to know that Grace and Henry will be provided for until their deaths," I say. "Beyond that, however . . ." I think of George at the docks in Bristol, emptying his pockets for the children, and speak from my heart. "I want my estate divided into two parts. One will go toward the founding of an orphanage in London. I want it to be named after my brother, and I want his paintings to find a permanent home there one day. The rest should go to my foster parents. I don't know what they'll do with such a sum, but I expect they will find a use for it—I anticipate them having many grandchildren."

"How lucky for them to have such a grateful foster child—though I do hope you outlive them by a fair measure. One day in the future, I hope we will sit together to change the terms of this will, to the benefit of your own children."

"I cannot imagine that just yet," I say. "There is so much death around me, new life is hard to contemplate."

He looks troubled, drinking the dregs of his tea. "You must miss your foster parents terribly. They sound very kind."

"Salt of the earth," I say, forcing a smile. "Though they had six children of their own, they took George and me in when we were orphaned. Nobody's life is easy in the country—we all worked hard on their ranch—but it was happy. We were never without love, we never went hungry, and they did not begrudge us anything."

"It sounds like you had a good life there."

"I did." I remember his strange response that night in London, when I asked about his family, and decide to try again. "Where does your own family live, Mr. Simpson? I don't recall whether you were brought up in London."

"I was not," he says lightly. "And I don't have family to speak of."

I'm about to ask more, when the screaming begins.

CHAPTER 15

M R. SIMPSON IS ON his feet before I am. "Wait here, Lady Katherine," he says urgently, striding from the room. I ignore him and follow close on his heels, pressing my hands to my thumping heart. We join the small stream of startled staff, rushing to the house's front lawn.

There we find the source of the screaming: Elsie, her head flopped down between her shoulders, flanked on either side by whispering maids. They're half carrying her limp body back into the house, though they look close to swooning themselves. "It was the Beast, I know it!" one shrills. As they pass me, I hear Elsie whimpering something, broken words coming out of her in a stream. "I thought it was Matt, oh God! I thought it was him, oh thank you God. . . ."

I look down at my hands, chilled with a premonition, a touch of second sight: They will soon be covered in blood. My eyes go, unwilling, to the two men laboring up the lawn. Matt and Henry, carrying something between them. The arrogant man with the black mustache walks alongside, twisting his hands together. "There's been an accident!" he yells, then repeats it twice more. Mr. Dowling is beside him, clapping a comforting arm about his shoulder in an effort to quiet his panic.

As I continue across the lawn, frightened but unable to stop, all I can see clearly are the men's broad black backs and bowed heads, but not their cargo. Then one of them stumbles a bit, and I see what I couldn't before, the thing held sagging between them. John, fighting against their arms. His body is rigid, pitching upward with pain, and his chest dark with blood.

"What's happened?" I cry. Mr. Simpson takes my elbow before I can run.

"Stand back, Katherine. Let them carry him."

I slump into him, and he circles his arm about me, his face stony and pale. We follow the group of men toward the house— poor Matt at John's feet, looking as though he could cry; Henry, cool and terse, supporting his shoulders. Again I see the mark of authority on his brow, the sharp efficiency of his soldiering days. "Not through that door!" he barks. "Carry him around to the servants' entrance."

"Are you mad? You're wasting time!" I say.

"Take her into the house, Mr. Simpson," Henry replies. "Don't look, Katherine."

To Mr. Simpson's credit, he does not listen. We follow the men into a scullery, where Mr. Dowling moves an aproned cook aside and quickly sweeps the large central table clear of the things set out for baking. John is laid across its floury surface. Several servants and men from the hunt press themselves against the far wall, watching, and Mr. Simpson pulls the curtains back from the windows as far as they'll go. Henry takes out a pocketknife and begins cutting John's shirt away from his chest.

The blood flows free and fast, obscuring the wound. "Katherine, move *back*," Henry says. Ignoring him, I grab a pile of clean washcloths from a sideboard. I press them hard into John's chest, ignoring his watery moan. But when he bares his teeth in pain, they're glazed in red, and I know that it's too late.

His eyes lock on mine, and the snatches of conversation around me fade into background noise, reaching my ears as if through a heavy fog.

"He was reloading his gun. . . ."

"Poor chap, should've known better than to hold it that way. . . ."

"Don't speak of it now, not in front of the young lady. . . ."

John's eyes roll white and wild in his head as I lean in toward him. "Just breathe," I whisper. "Lie quiet." His eyes are calming now, but I can see, too, that their light is dying away. He raises an arm, I think to touch me, then brings it down to rest at the pocket of his peeled-back coat. I clasp the other, flopping uselessly near his throat. Our noses nearly touch. His lips move again, over blood-slicked teeth, and his eyes pulse with terror and urgency. Silently he mouths something, then gives a weak shudder, and is gone.

Nobody speaks for a long moment. When I step back, blood is caked on my black dress and smeared over my skin. With horror I remember that my brother had to breathe his last breath alone. I offer up a quick prayer of thanksgiving that I was able to save John from that fate.

The other men, their faces grave, have moved outside to smoke with shaking hands. Henry leans forward onto balled fists at John's side, his face turned down toward the table.

"How did this happen?" asks Mr. Dowling, his voice half-solicitous and half-formal, falling smoothly into his role as magistrate.

Henry stands upright, running one hand hard across his face. "We were coming up on a covey," he says dully. "I'd run ahead of him to gain a better position. I fired, I missed, I called back to John for another gun. I heard a shot go off below, but did not immediately turn. I thought perhaps he'd tried for something himself. He said no word, made no sound. When I turned back, he was on the ground." His voice breaks. "God knows how this could have happened. The boy's been loading guns as long as he's been riding horses."

Wearily, avoiding my gaze, he gestures to Mr. Simpson. "Sir, will you help me move him to the west wing? It's the coldest part of the house."

Before I can wince at the familiar words, something slips from John's pocket and hits the ground with a cold clatter. I see that it fell from the pocket his hand had gestured toward, moments before he slipped away. Mr. Simpson stoops low to inspect the thing without touching it, and as I watch, the whole line of his body goes absolutely still.

He turns shocked eyes on me. "Katherine, please look at this thing." I swipe the ready tears from my eyes and kneel down beside him. A gold pocket watch lies on the ground, engraved in sweeping script: *G.R.*

In a flash, I see my father, lit by the amber light of memory, winding the watch with careful pride. "My God," I breathe. Henry crowds in at my shoulder, and I hear his breath catch.

"Everyone, leave the room," he says. "All but you, Mr. Simpson, and you, Mr. Dowling." Gape-mouthed servants file out of the room, some knuckling at their eyes or openly weeping.

Henry turns to the three of us that remain, his jaw tight. "I must insist that the news of this discovery not leave Walthingham Hall. Two such tragedies in close succession, it is almost more than I can bear. But this new finding . . . Katherine, can you confirm that this is your brother's watch?"

"Yes," I whisper. "He carried it with him always. It belonged to our father—his name was George, too."

"Good God, Henry," Mr. Dowling says heavily. "Could it be that this servant had a hand in the death of the heir?"

Henry's eyes flash to mine, followed by Mr. Dowling's. "Lady Randolph, I hope that you may forgive me one day," says the magistrate, "for dismissing your fears out of hand."

I nod, holding my cold fingers out to meet his. "Of course I do, sir."

My suspicions have been borne out at last, my fears vindicated. But it's an empty triumph. A cold revulsion takes hold in the pit of my stomach—could it be that the same hands that held me the night before, that slid hotly over my skin, so recently ended my brother's life?

CHAPTER 16

HENRY SENDS MATT to Bath in pursuit of the coroner, and Mr. Dowling leads several men through the halls to John's room, where they will search for other effects of my brother's. Alone in the scullery, I take a damp cloth to the watch, swirling away clots of dried red. The wan light through the windows illuminates my haggard hands, and the air smells of pipe smoke, blood, and damp feathers—one of the men hung a row of broken grouse overhead. No point in wasting the meat, of course, but the act seems terribly petty. As I remove the final smudge, I turn the watch over to inspect its motionless hands. My father wound his watch daily. But now when I try to do the same, the mechanism won't work.

My pain, my rage is focused on the sullied watch—a family heirloom that I can never again take pleasure in. I bring my hand back to throw it, but the false drama of the gesture turns my stomach. Resigned, I tuck it away into my pocket, to be fixed another day.

Would John have done this thing? What motive could he possibly have had? I remember George and me passing him in the hall just before the ball—was George's cool nod an affront? Did John think us pretenders to our wealth, jumped-up peasants? George could be too quick and cocky for his own good. Perhaps he said something to anger John—perhaps there was an argument that got out of hand. I press my forehead into my cold hands.

A shadow in the doorway says my name, then steps forward into the thin daylight. It's Elsie. "They want you in the parlor, my lady," she says, her voice a white whisper. Her face is unreadable through her shock. Whatever she might have felt toward the rumored father of her sister's child, she couldn't have longed for this. I push the thought away. Whether John had ruined a girl and then abandoned her could hardly matter now. He would account for it in a higher court than that of my own mind.

In the parlor I find my cousins and William Simpson. Though Henry has changed into a clean shirtfront, he has offered nothing to Mr. Simpson, who sits quietly in a shirt stained with blood.

Grace's voice is tinged with hysteria. "I never did trust John, and I was always glad to say so. Even before the talk surrounding the incident with that girl, I thought he was a bad apple. Oh, the trials of finding good help!" She threw up her hands in theatrical supplication, and I fight back a tide of contempt. Two men dead, and she talks of the troubles in staffing Walthingham.

139

Her brother reaches out his arm to both comfort and quiet her. "There is no help in speaking ill of the dead, sister—though I cannot express my pain at my oversight, in letting such a criminal insinuate himself into life at Walthingham Hall. His father was a very decent man, and it was for his sake that I never fired the son. I've long suspected him of stealing from the house, and just yesterday confronted him about it. I'm surprised the man did not sneak away in the night."

With a jolt, I realize that this must be the confrontation I witnessed as I exited the woods after my run-in with McAllister. John had lied so ably to me when asked about their argument. Had all of our interactions been a lie? I'm mute with shame at the way I was taken in, until I remember something else.

"Henry, the day after the ball I overhead John arguing with two men in our front hall. They were asking to speak with you, but he turned them away."

"Asking to speak with *me*? Perhaps they meant to uncover some truth about him to me—no doubt the men were contacts of his, blackmailers of some sort. Like falls in with like."

"Is it possible, sir, that John's death was not an accident?" The cold clarity of Mr. Simpson's voice cuts through the fog of my thoughts.

"McAllister," I breathe. "He knows the woods better than anyone. And I know that John did not like him." I blush, hoping no one will ask how I came to possess this knowledge.

Henry mulls this a moment. "It's possible, I suppose. Not likely—I grew up in these woods myself, and I know them just as well as Mr. McAllister. I doubt he could have been near without my detecting him. Though it's true that the man never got on with John *or* his father."

Mr. Simpson speaks with unexpected force. "Just because a man has been accused of poaching does not mean he would kill someone in cowardly cold blood."

Before Henry can respond, Mr. Dowling enters the room, trailed by two men. "There's a note," he says briefly, holding something out to Henry. My heart thumps. Mr. Simpson, sitting beside me, notices my stiffened posture. "Are you all right, Katherine?" he asks. I nod in silence as Henry begins to read the letter aloud.

> To all those touched by my sins,
>
> Having done a terrible thing and being regretful for it, I mean to take my own life. The heir of Walthingham Hall, my birthplace and home, came at me in the stables with an accusation that I stole the silver. I did do that crime, but my anger at being found out was such that I committed another: I killed George Randolph with a blow to the head, using the hoofpick I held in my hand. It were not in anger but in fear that I did this, and I cannot live to know my sins another day.
>
> Forgive me, forgive me. May God forgive me.
> John Hayes

I rise and move to Henry's shoulder, quickly skimming the letter's contents. It strikes me as wrong in every respect. How could John possibly have managed such writing? I struggle to express myself without giving anything away. "This note is far beyond the abilities of a footman, don't you think?"

Grace looks at me with pity over the back of the couch. In her expression I see that I needn't have hidden my ink-stained dress—Mr. Carrick has told her all. She hooks cold fingers about my arm. "It wouldn't be the first time a man has lied about his abilities," she murmurs, "to suit the vanities of a young girl."

I snatch my arm back and glance toward Mr. Simpson, who seems, thankfully, too absorbed in thought to have heard her.

"Perhaps Lady Katherine is right," he says, his brow puckered with concern. "I believe I've met the man once or twice, and such expression does not sit easily with my understanding of him."

Henry tuts. "Mr. Simpson, please. Katherine has no need of more fanciful conspiracies to distract her tired mind."

Mr. Simpson and I spring from our seats simultaneously, but he speaks before I can. "Fanciful conspiracies! Perhaps we should give the lady more credence. It seems she was correct in her belief that her brother's death was foul play."

Still seated, Henry watches the man with bored eyes. "Perhaps there will come a time when we need the advice of a solicitor on this matter," he says with acid politeness. "Until then, however, you may keep your opinions to yourself. I shall call for Carrick to show you out."

I remain standing. "There's no need of Mr. Carrick. I'll see Mr. Simpson to the door myself."

I stalk out of the room, worrying only that Mr. Dowling

may think me impolite. It brings on an unwelcome realization: that Mr. Simpson is made of far better stuff than my own surviving family. He follows me to the front of the house without speaking, his quiet presence steady at my back. At the door, I place my hand lightly on his arm. "Thank you, sir, for speaking on my behalf. I was ready to do so myself, but I'm afraid anger would have made a mess of my meaning." I look down at the crusted red of his shirtfront, feeling ashamed. "Please allow me to bring you something fresh to wear. You cannot ride out in that shirt."

He gazes back at me, and I sense that he wants to say something but cannot or will not find the words. After a lingering pause, he speaks. "Thank you, but I am beholden enough to Walthingham as it is. Lady Katherine, I remain at your service. I return to London tomorrow, but please know that I will give you my counsel freely and at any time."

I can hardly bear to look into the rich blue of his eyes, burning with a passion that belies the spare politeness of his words.

Must he always retreat behind this veil of propriety, through which I'm allowed only the most incomplete glimpses? It makes me want to shake him and his damnable decorum by the shoulders. How would he react if I kissed him the way John kissed me? Would he push me away, or would he respond to my touch, as he did in my dream?

I grow hot with a sudden belief that he can read the thoughts on my face. His last words are oddly loaded.

"I await your instructions, Lady Katherine. If you should have need of me, I tell you again: I will be there to help you at once." He clasps my ungloved hand briefly in his larger, warm one, before turning to depart.

For a long time after he is gone, I find my mind returning to his last words, and to the gentle pressure of his palm against mine. I drift back to the morning room and gaze up at the painting of my grandfather. In all his time as steward of Walthingham Hall, was there ever such a bloody period as this one? Or was the removal of my father's branch from the family tree the cruelest cut of his era?

I long to return to the first time Mr. Simpson and I stood here in the half-light, when my most serious concern was how high society would take to me. My brother alive, my friendship with Jane fresh and new, and John alive, not a murderer, just a callow footman I need not think of.

In the absence of Jane to talk to, I'm grateful to find Stella in my room, whining beneath the bed.

"Poor thing," I murmur, coaxing her out. Walthingham smells like blood and horses today, and it must have sent her scurrying. I pull her into my lap and decide that it's time to finally write my letter.

Among the jumble of my writing desk, I find the bright, heedless note I'd begun penning the day after the ball, while my brother's broken body lay less than a mile away. Its blithe, cocky sentiments now fill me with shame. Ripping it into a dozen pieces, I lay out a sheet of fresh paper and begin again.

Dear Aunt Lila and Uncle Edward,

I'm deeply sorry for my silence these past weeks.
Though I came here to claim a home and a family,

I find that I am more alone than ever. I have many events to recount, but I wish to do so in person. For now, you must know only two things: One, that my brother is dead, a tragedy compounded by its being the result of foul play. Two, that by the time you read this letter, I will be on my way home. . . .

CHAPTER 17

FOR THE FIRST time in days I do not dream. When I come to with a thumping heart in the middle of the night, I'm not sure at first what's woken me.

Then, far away, I hear a series of barks, followed by a terrible squeal. Thrusting my arms into the covers, I realize Stella is not beside me.

A moment later, I'm on the landing. I barely recall how I got there, how I threw on a robe and ran headlong into the black of the hall. A sleepy blonde maid is beside me, rubbing her eyes and staring down into the dark pit of the stairs. "Did you hear that sound?" she asks tremulously. Then, seeing to whom she's speaking, she amends herself. "But I'm sure it was nothing, my lady."

"May I?" I say. She hands me her lantern, then curtsies and melts back into the unlit hall. My bare feet are cold and careful against the marble steps; as I descend I hear voices below, and I see the wavering light of candles.

When I reach the bottom step, the housekeeper's face swims into view, pale beneath her red hair. "You should be abed, my lady. The servants will locate the source of the noise."

"It was my dog, Mrs. Whiting, I'm sure of it. I want to help them find her; she must be hurt."

She shakes her head but lets me pass. I move softly in my circle of lamplight. Servants stir in the doorways along my path, though none speak to me. A draft teases my ankles, and instinctively I change course, heading toward the west wing.

Then a shout breaks the hush—sure enough, it comes from the west, where John's body lies. The wing has become a mortuary.

The door in the temporary wall already hangs open, and I move swiftly past the sheeted furniture, following the low hum of voices to a small room at the house's outer edge. When I enter, I see my cousin standing at the window looking down, his form outlined in moonlight. Elsie stands with a knot of other servants near the door, and attempts to catch my sleeve as I pass.

"Lady Katherine . . ." she breathes.

Henry turns swiftly, his face contorted. "Don't look," he says. I ignore him, pressing a hand to my mouth to gag the scream I feel gathering strength in my chest.

The window's open, and an icy breeze ghosts around me, lifting tendrils of damp hair from my brow. I grip the sill and look down. There, below the window, lies Stella's small body, still in the silvery light and matted with blood.

"This was not an accident," I say immediately.

"Her neck is broken," says Henry briefly. "Someone broke her neck," he repeats, his voice filled with horror.

"Or some*thing*," says Elsie, behind me.

Henry turns sharply, fists clenched. "For the last time, there is no Beast of Walthingham." His eyes are black pools in the lamplight. "And the next person who implies otherwise will be removed from the estate at once, without back wages."

"Please, someone get my dog," I say. I can't stop shivering, despite my robe. Henry takes my arm and forces me to a chair, where I sit helplessly, waiting for Stella's body to be brought inside.

Long moments tick by, elastic and immeasurable in the wavering light, with everyone staring at me, waiting to see whether I'll break. I make my hands into tight balls and refuse to meet their eyes. If John began this horror by killing my brother, what does it mean that his own death hasn't stopped it? I think again of the letter he supposedly wrote—and the wavering words he produced in our lesson together.

Finally, the man Henry sent out returns. He looks vaguely familiar—I think he's the estate's smith. My dog is tiny in his arms. "She's bloody, miss," he says apologetically. "You don't want to hold her with that nice dress."

"It's just a robe. Give her to me."

I cradle the cool little body in my arms. She's even smaller in death—a true runt. "Henry," I say, "McAllister did this. He threatened her, and now he's made good on it. That man killed my dog."

"That's not possible. He wouldn't dare come closer in than that old lodge, and he certainly couldn't get into the house."

"I saw someone a few nights ago, standing at the tree line,"

I say. "Who else could it be? Who else would be so cruel as to harm a helpless dog?"

"But that wouldn't explain why the window was open." Mrs. Whiting speaks from the doorway. "I personally check the windows each night, and I'm certain this one was latched and locked when I did my rounds. There's no question but that it was opened from the inside."

There's a cool challenge in her voice, and I'm unsure at whom it's directed. My own voice is steely in response. "Mrs. Whiting, I have no doubt that man could enter any room of this house if he wished to. This wing is the least secure part of the estate! Stella startled him, and now she's paid the price."

"Mr. McAllister is not a bogeyman, Lady Katherine, capable of popping in and out without consequence," she responds tartly. "This house is well secured nightly, by myself."

"Mrs. Whiting, Katherine is not disparaging your work," says Henry. "All of us must be vigilant, but now, please return to your beds. I think I need not remind you that what happens at Walthingham Hall is not to be spoken of beyond the estate."

As the servants file out, led by a quietly furious Mrs. Whiting, he kneels before me and attempts to ease Stella from my arms. "Katherine, please allow me to take her. I'll bury her somewhere nice for you—beneath a flowering tree, perhaps. She was your friend; I think you'll want to visit her sometimes." His tone is kind but brisk. As with George's death, Henry wishes to push Stella's aside, to clean up after it and move on.

I'm holding her tight to me, still unwilling to give her up, when he grabs my hand tightly. "You don't deserve this," he says, his voice grim. "Let me do what I can to make it right."

He mistakes my surprised stillness for surrender, and pulls my dog away. When he's limped softly from the room, moving carefully with his little burden, Elsie moves to my side. "I can sleep in your room tonight, Lady Katherine," she offers.

I nod wordlessly. I feel too numb to do anything but accept.

CHAPTER 18

POOR ELSIE—OUR heads barely touch our pillows. I keep her awake for hours, helping me pack and sort my things, until the birds below begin to stir and twitter in the first gray light of morning. I'm more determined than ever to put this place, which has brought me nothing but misery, behind me. At times Elsie's eyes fill with tears, though she does not try to dissuade me from leaving—I wonder whether she will miss me, or my protection. I can't imagine she'll stay in my aunt's employ for long once I'm gone, but I do not have the energy to feel guilt over this.

Finally, I lie across my rumpled bed, and Elsie drapes herself over a low chaise to catch an hour of sleep before dawn truly arrives. When I wake, it's with sandy eyes and a sharp resolve that propels me from my bed, despite the poisonous headache I'm staggering under.

I leave Elsie where she lies, knowing another maid will catch her there before Mrs. Whiting does, and take the small satchel I've filled with my most important effects for my journey. My old blue trunk is packed to the brim with pretty things for Anna and Aunt Lila, and the sturdier of my new clothes for me. The restlessness that's been coursing through me for days now has shape and purpose. As I walk to the first floor, looking for an early-rising footman to help me with my trunk, I feel as though I'm truly breathing for the first time since before the funeral.

I regret only that I must leave George's body behind. I try to take comfort in his immediate affinity for England, though it seems wrong that his body wasn't laid beside our parents'. My mind is so far ahead, already lingering on the faces of those I'll be returning to in Virginia, that it's a shock to come upon Henry pacing in the wan light of the foyer, his face care-lined but his eyes alive with purpose. His bad hip rolls stiffly in its socket as he turns, catching sight of me.

"You look as though you're waiting for someone, cousin," I say.

"That's because I am." His gaze wanders over the satchel hanging from my hand, but he does not speak the question I can see in his eyes. "I haven't slept, Katherine. My mind was spinning; I couldn't close my eyes. Forgive me, but I must speak to you about something of great importance, at once."

I close my eyes, seeing myself on the coach to Bristol, then, finally, on the next ship home to America. "I share your troubles, Henry. I slept only an hour, and must unburden myself to you as well."

His eyes, strangely avid, racing from my eyes, to my mouth,

and back again, light up at these words. "Can this be true, Katherine? Could it be we're haunted by the same thoughts?"

"I doubt it very much, cousin . . ." I begin, but to my dismay, he's already taking my free hand in his, then lowering himself gingerly to one knee.

The light falls on his tired face, and as he speaks he looks older than I've ever seen him. "Katherine Randolph, I have loved you since the moment I saw you. I couldn't speak sooner without dishonoring the memory of your brother, but I can keep quiet no longer. Would you bless me with your hand in marriage?"

"Oh! Henry, I . . ." I can't think of anything but Jane. This isn't right at all, and if it weren't for the genuine supplication in Henry's face, I would assume they were both pulling some sick ruse on me. I stand in dumb absorption, staring down at him. His fair hair is losing color at the sides, going slowly to silver. When he's nervous, as he is now, his hands have a fine tremor. And his eyes, which I thought were brown, are actually shot through with green. It gives them a distant look. He's quite dashing still, and must have cut a swath through the hearts of society women when he was young— before the war. I have never had such an opportunity to study him as I do now, as Henry has always seemed distant to me, moving through the house with an authoritative air, the curdled victory of his military service still hanging on him like a tarnished badge. Before I can speak again, Henry stumbles on, unable to bear my silent scrutiny.

"These last few weeks have taught me that nothing is certain, that life is sacred—a lesson I knew better once but had nearly forgotten. My sister urged me to wait until you're a bit older . . . but why deny ourselves the happiness we can give to each other?" He ends this little speech with a flourish, as though he's successfully removed the final obstacle to our shared happiness.

He's waiting in pained silence for me to reply, but my mind hums, empty. He speaks as though I've said yes, as though he's certain of my love, but I've given him no such commitment. And Jane—what of her? They are in love, aren't they? I've seen it with my own eyes. She has told me of their plans.

"This is very sudden, cousin," I say faintly.

With a pained grimace he tries to cover with a smile, he brings himself back to standing. "You know me to be a man of action." Now, standing over me, he is Henry again, distant and cool. It gives me the power to speak without stumbling.

"I think," I say, "that I need time to consider. I would like time to think."

Oh, Jane. Poor, poor Jane . . .

"Yes, of course." Again he takes my unresponsive hand. "I see that you are planning on going out today. If you're traveling to the churchyard to visit your poor brother, I would be happy to accompany you. I would have liked to ask his blessing for my proposal."

The way he falls so easily into bluff charm turns me cold. "No," I lie quickly. "I was planning to see Jane."

Does something flicker in his eyes at the sound of her name, or is it my imagination? Certainly his smile does not dim as he presses his mouth gently to my gloved hand. "I await your response, Katherine. Please do not leave me in anticipation for long."

In the absence of John, Matt drives me into Bath. Perhaps they won't make him leave after all—despite Henry's command, word will get out about John's death. Between that and rumors of the Beast, many servants will be too frightened even to apply at Walthingham. I allow myself a moment's dark satisfaction, imagining Grace fumbling through the preparation of her own toilette. Without servants to help her, she'd starve in a week.

The look on my face tells Matt that I do not wish to speak, and the ride is swift and silent. I look back at the great house just once, remembering how I admired it the first time I saw it. Now it seems to me a house of hidden horrors, an unlooked-for inheritance that turned quickly into a curse.

The landscape is not nearly as pretty with the snow melted away, and I barely note a twig of it. My lie to Henry quickly became a dreaded errand—I must put off my departure for one more day, to tell my friend of Henry's proposal. My mind races, recalling her tender words on the frozen lawn just after the ball, and the longing looks I've seen pass between them. Surely she could not have imagined his regard for her? Was their romance only in her mind, born of Henry's easy charm and good humor? He has a courtly way about him that could be misconstrued. I cannot believe him to be so villainous as to give her false hopes—not intentionally.

All of my apprehensions cannot make our journey any longer than it is, and we arrive sooner than I'd like. I unlatch the door with frozen fingers and step down. In my mind's eye I imagine Jane at a window above, watching my arrival and anticipating a pleasant afternoon. To stretch this illusion, I make my steps to the door as short and slow as I can, feeling Matt's curious eyes boring into my back. With a shaky breath, I bring down the door knocker.

The door is flung open nearly at once by an elderly butler, and I'm shown into the front hall. I keep my head down as I'm announced, watching my boots leave small pools of muck on the entrance carpet.

Finally, I'm called into the library, a room that smells of leather and pipe smoke and is very clearly the province of Mr. Dowling. He's quite at his leisure in the middle of it, sitting behind a broad desk. A teacup lies atop a stack of papers close by his hand, surrounded by overlapping brown rings, and a book is splayed open across his great chest. He looks at me kindly over half-glasses.

"Lady Katherine. It's wonderful to see you on your feet, child, despite the blow that has once again befallen Walthingham. Jane is visiting friends, but she'll be back within the hour. You'll take a nice cup with me while we wait for her."

I can't help but smile at Mr. Dowling, and at the comfort of this cozy room. It speaks clearly of the enforced bachelorhood of the not-so-old widower. Soon I'm warming my hands around a cup of hot English tea, fragrant with bergamot and honey.

Though he tries to distract me with bits of gossip, even pushing a green-bound volume of poems across the table, recommending that I take it with me when I go, my mood soon moves us both to ruminative silence.

"Mr. Dowling, I'm a poor companion today," I say apologetically. "But as we have a moment to speak, I must ask you again about your thoughts on Mr. McAllister. The note John left, it . . . it seems too easy, too unlikely. He seemed such a simple, good man to me, and McAllister such a menace—we know him to be a thief, and to have great knowledge of the woods about Walthingham—"

He cuts me off gently, leaning across to take the teacup from my gesturing hand. "I have found, my dear, that the simplest explanations are always the best. You must not look for a scandal when the real answer has already been presented to you."

He sighs, settling heavily back into his chair. "McAllister has long been an outsider here—even in the eyes of his own family. He had a wife and child once, but they left him years ago. No one can even say where he lives, now that he no longer has that cottage on the estate."

"Don't you see?" I say. "What kind of man drives away his own wife and child? And does not try to go after them?"

"I believe he did, actually—he took a leave of absence from your grandfather's estate for a period of time. When he returned, he was more reclusive than ever. A man like that is a man who knows how to stay hidden. No matter his personal grudges—and I do not doubt that he has them—I don't believe that he would sacrifice the anonymity he enjoys now. The man lives an animal's life: solitary, close to the land. He would not endanger what small safeties he's carved out for himself."

From the hall we hear the cheerful clatter of Jane's approach. Her father's face flushes with pleasure as she enters—windblown, cheeks pink with cold. I look down at myself, thinner than before and wrapped in my mourning blacks. Jane is vibrant and positively blooming, though she mutes her enthusiasm for my sake, coming forward to take my hands.

"I'm so pleased to see you, Katherine—I just sent a note to Walthingham Hall, after my father told me what happened to John. It's a terrible thing, and we'll be very happy to keep you here as long as you'd like to stay. It might do you good to be away from the estate for a bit."

Her effusive kindness washes over me, intensifying my shame. Though I did nothing wrong, the weight of Henry's betrayal seems to linger on my skin.

Jane notices that her father has stealthily picked up his book again, side-eyeing its pages longingly, and suggests that we go into her sitting room.

"Thank you for the tea, Mr. Dowling," I say, following Jane from the room. In that moment I feel as if in the thrall of a petite jailer leading me to the guillotine.

In her sitting room she pulls me onto a pale blue love seat, tucking her legs up under her so our knees touch. It's the kind of pose that Anna, my best friend in Virginia, would affect before an hour of gossip. I chafe under the expectation of friendly intimacy, feeling as if I could cry.

She begins speaking before I can. "First I must apologize for not coming to the hunt that day, though I know you wished it."

"No, please don't worry about that now. Jane, I must tell you something. It's about my cousin—it's about Henry. He asked me something this morning, and I came straight here to tell you about it. . . ."

She cuts me off, her face going dreamy. "He's exactly the reason I didn't come that day. You see, I could not bear to see him and my father side by side—I'm sure my face would have given it all away!"

"I don't understand. Given what away?"

Her eyes flash with coy mischief. "You see, my father is leaving Bath for business very soon, and Henry and I plan on spending the day together—alone. My father often travels. Just after your arrival, in fact, Henry and I managed to spend an afternoon in an inn outside of Wells. One of those places where only travelers go. He told them we were man and wife!" She hides her face in her hands, as though ashamed, but I see her smile peeping out from behind her fingers.

My mouth drops as I catch her meaning. If Jane has compromised herself for my heartless cousin, there can be no doubt of his wickedness. I remember his words from this morning: *Katherine Randolph, I have loved you since the moment I saw you.* Yet, days after meeting me, he was stealing the honor of a lovely girl in a cheap inn.

Jane is not too stricken with love to miss the horrified expression on my face. "Katherine, it's all right. Henry is coming here on my father's return, to finally ask for my hand!" The words tumble out of her; I can tell she's long been wishing to say them.

And suddenly, I cannot find the words to tell her that the man she's pinned her hopes on, that she's already given herself to, is so unfaithful. "Are you certain that he's the right husband for you?" I blurt out, sudden and too loud.

Her face, so radiant and trusting, shuts tight as a fist. "What are you talking about?" she says.

My throat is dry; I can barely swallow. "I only mean . . . Don't you think he's a bit . . . *old* for you?"

"Why are you saying this?" she cries, propelling her body as far back across the love seat as it can go. "You know how I feel about him—I've made him a promise!"

I reach for her hand, foolishly, and she snatches it back. "Explain yourself, Katherine. What has happened to change your affections toward me?"

"Jane, please. I feel the same toward you as ever—only, I must tell you something. This morning, Henry . . . he asked for my hand. In marriage. I never wanted it, and I didn't have any idea that he would, I just . . ."

Her hand connects smartly with my cheek, shocking me into silence. "How *dare you*?" she spits, her pretty doll's face contorted behind sudden tears.

I hold my throbbing cheek in silence. There's nothing I can say to alleviate her pain.

Mr. Dowling crashes into the room, red-faced and puffing. "Good lord, girls, do I hear weeping?" He stops speaking when he sees us, my body hunched into itself and Jane burying her face in pillows, her shoulders shaking with sobs.

"What has happened here?" he asks softly.

"It's my fault," I whisper. "I'll go—I must go at once."

As I rush toward the entrance, I hear Jane tearfully demanding that her father leave her alone. I don't stay to hear his response, but he must have listened: He joins me in the foyer a moment later, where I'm waiting miserably for the butler to bring my things.

"Girls often argue, and they often make up," he says, rubbing his forehead in sad perplexity. "Though I don't claim to understand it, I'm sure you two will be bosom friends again before your next ball together."

I nod in silence, taking pity on a man who must wish very much for the advice of his wife today. And before I leave Jane's home for the final time, I ask her father for a certain address. He seems surprised but acquiesces. I don't worry whether my request makes me seem less of a lady in his eyes—in a day or two, it won't matter what anyone in this country thinks of me.

CHAPTER 19

I ASK MATT TO drop me off a few streets from my destination, so that I might walk through the busy streets of Bath a final time. Though the day is fine, cold and bright, the golden stone of the buildings has lost its charm for me. My eyes long to rest on Virginia's rustling vistas of hickory and oak, to breathe air fragrant with pine sap instead of smoke and crowds.

When I reach the address given to me by Mr. Dowling, it's much as I imagined it: a cozy three-story brick house, unadorned but well kept. A very young maid in a starched cap answers my knock.

"My name is Katherine Simpson; I am Mr. William Simpson's cousin," I say coolly. "Is he in?"

"He is, ma'am."

"Would you please show me to his rooms at once? No need to announce me—he's expecting this visit."

She surveys my clothing, evidently debating whether I am who I say I am. "Female guests are not allowed beyond the parlor," she says in a thick country accent, then flashes her dimples at me. "But the master of the house is away, and if you're Mr. Simpson's cousin I see no harm in it."

I nod slightly, feeling an uncomfortable stab of jealousy toward this pretty maid, then follow her through a hallway redolent with cooking smells. She leads me up an uncarpeted flight of stairs, and then raps sharply on the first door that we come to.

There's a rustle and scrape from within, as of papers put aside and a chair pushed back, then Mr. Simpson appears at the door. He's in a white shirt, the collar unbuttoned, and spectacles sit on his nose. He runs a hand through his mussed dark hair and snatches the spectacles from his face, tucking them into his pocket. "Lady Katherine!"

The maid turns to me in frank curiosity as my cheeks burn red. "Thank you, Mary," Mr. Simpson says hurriedly. His face seems to be wavering between embarrassment and something else, finally settling into his customary seriousness. "You've caught me at lunch." The plate on the table behind him holds watery stew and a trencher of bread—farm food.

"Perhaps I might eat with you?" I ask.

He nods uncertainly. "Mary, would you please bring up another portion?" As she curtsies and walks pertly away, he turns to me. "Has something happened? Are you all right?"

I hesitate a moment, then shake my head. "I'm not. But perhaps I shouldn't have come here—I don't wish to put you in the way of gossip." I make myself look into his eyes. "I told her I was your cousin."

"Cousin or not, this visit isn't entirely proper," he says, his gaze never leaving mine. "But I'm very glad to see you."

For a moment we stand in the middle of the room, looking at each other. My black skirts over crinolines seem to cover half the floor, and I feel too shy to remove my hat.

Finally, he reaches his hand out toward mine. "Would you like to—" he begins, and then Mary returns bearing a covered plate, and tea in a chipped cup.

As she sets the table, taking far longer than she needs to, I look around the room. It's simple and clean, comfortably cluttered with books and papers. I spy an alcove at the rear, through which a bed with smooth white sheets can be seen. I see Mr. Simpson following my gaze, and swiftly turn my eyes to the floor.

With a curtsy, Mary withdraws again. Mr. Simpson picks up his teacup and raises a brow. "Would you like to remove your hat, Lady Katherine?" he says.

"You should call me Kat," I reply. "Now more than ever. I'm here because I mean to sell Walthingham Hall."

His hand pauses in midair a moment before he brings it up the rest of the way and swigs the remainder of his tea. "But why?" he says, his jaw tight.

I shift under the intensity of his stare. "Surely you can guess, sir."

"But to give up your home . . . Where would you live?"

"It's not my home," I say quietly. "It never has been."

He slaps his cup onto the table and moves closer to me. "Am I understanding your intent, Lady Katherine? Do you mean to leave England?"

There's a tremor in his voice that makes it difficult for me to speak. "I do. Please understand that I must."

"But you can't go," he says quickly. "I mean, you mustn't. Even without your house, you have your title. Your brother's exhibition is coming up; we must navigate the sale of his paintings together, and the founding of the orphanage you spoke of." His voice is filled with urgency.

"Mr. Simpson, you cannot talk me out of returning. Please don't try. I'll still bestow money for the orphanage—I trust you to see to its founding, and will pay you well to do so. But please do what you must to begin the sale of Walthingham. As soon as possible." I've spoken more loudly than I need to, and the silence that follows my words is thick.

Finally, he shakes his head. "If that is what you wish, then I'll help you. But, Katherine: You're still under the guardianship of your cousin. He will need to sign the deed of sale, and you won't see the money until two years from now, when you become independent."

"I can wait. I can work. I'll want for nothing in Virginia."

"But you've changed," he says simply. "You may find, when you arrive, that the place is the same, that your family loves you as well as ever. But *you'll* be different. Too different, I fear, to return to your former life."

I step toward him, searching his face. "Why do you say these things to me? What good can it do you to be cruel?"

"Cruel!" He reaches out and grabs my hand, his touch sending a bolt through me. "I swear that isn't my intent. I speak from experience—I want only to save you pain, if I can. . . ."

His face is closer to mine than it's ever been. My heart stutters as he moves his hand to my shoulder, then my neck, cupping the hollow there. "There are people here who care about you," he says. "Who have come to *more* than care for you . . ."

Then his fingers find my still-reddened cheek. As he touches the raw skin there, I see Jane's face, in the instant before the slap. Her rage, her pain—all caused by me, by my unlucky arrival in England.

I close my eyes and jerk my head away, and just like that Mr. Simpson's hand falls away. When I open my eyes again, he's standing straight and proud. He looks again like the man he was during our earliest acquaintance, his tenderness replaced with stiff embarrassment.

"I'm going back to America," I say.

"Yes, I know. I know that you must."

"Getting close to you . . . it will only cause both of us pain."

"Yes, my lady. You're right. Forgive me for . . . for momentarily imagining otherwise."

I shake my head helplessly. "I'm happy that you could. That anyone could want to be close with me now, after all that's happened—it means more than I can say."

He still watches his hands. "You aren't to blame for what's happened since you arrived here. Please believe this."

My heart is in my throat as I reach into my purse and pull out my brother's watch. Though the blood has been cleaned away, I'll always see it, splattering the thing's fine face. "Here." I push it toward him, across the table. "I want you to keep this."

He looks at the watch as though afraid to touch it. "I could not."

"Please," I say. "Something to remember me by."

He stands up, surprised. "Lady Katherine . . . *Kat* . . . I'll need no help remembering you, and I can't accept such a valuable gift."

"You must," I insist, standing up to face him. "It's broken, but you can have it fixed. I'd like to think of it here, in your possession."

Finally, he folds his hand over the watch, and then tucks it away into his pocket. "Thank you," he says.

I step close to him and rise onto my toes, pressing my lips to his cheek. I inhale his good, clean scent for a moment. "Good-bye, William," I whisper, then hurry from the room.

It's as much as I can do to compose myself before allowing the housemaid to see me out—cousin or not, there will be gossip if I'm seen running from a gentleman's lodgings in tears.

Walking back toward the coach, I feel that my last tether to this place has been cut. But it doesn't make me feel free—just empty. *I should have kissed him properly*, I think. *What could it matter now?* So lost am I in thoughts of him, of the other ways our parting might have unfolded, that I run directly into the rough coat of a man traveling in the opposite direction. As I raise my arms in brief apology, not wishing to be detained, he grips them tight at the elbows.

I look up, full into his face, and see with a start that he is not a stranger. He's the rail-thin intruder I overheard John arguing with at Walthingham Hall, the morning after the ball. His blue eyes hold mine with smiling menace.

"Take your hands off me at once!" I cry.

Then another hand clamps around my mouth, and an arm crushes me at the waist. A voice from behind hisses in my ear.

"You'll want to keep your voice down, Lady Katherine. This can be quick or not, but screaming won't help you either way."

CHAPTER 20

M Y CAPTOR PULLS me back into an alleyway, my boots kicking and clattering over loose stones. The skinny man keeps a watch to either side, and then follows us. He tilts his hand to show me the knife in it, glinting.

I'm shoved against a moldering brick wall, still clamped to the second man's chest. Twisting to see his face, I accidentally bite down on my tongue. The sudden taste of metal is sharp against my teeth, and the damp scent of decaying plaster makes me woozy—but I've identified him: He's the squat, brutal-looking one who accompanied the tall man to Walthingham Hall.

My eyes keep traveling of their own accord to the knife, and I see that the hand gripping it is freshly bandaged. I gawk at it for a moment before I'm overcome with the gut-punched recognition of my own stupidity. All the time I'd been accusing old McAllister, insisting he be questioned, I'd paid no mind to the clearer threat.

"It was you, wasn't it?" I breathe, glaring at the tall man incredulously. "You who've been lurking around Walthingham—you who Stella got a bite out of, before you managed to kill her. Thank God for that, at least." I spit a mouthful of copper at his feet, too angry to be afraid.

Tall laughs, in a way that does not involve his flat blue eyes. "Spirited, isn't she?" he says. "It's lucky for you that our employer has no interest in teaching uppity girls about the world and their place in it. Though my friend here would be happy to make the lesson on his own, were I to request it." His fat companion holds me in an unshifting grip, showing no inclination to speak again.

And just like that, all the humor slides from Tall's face. "But here's what my employer *does* want: his money. All of it, up front, and fast."

"I don't know why you're demanding it from me. You're masons, are you not? Why not settle your accounts with the household?"

"Oh, she's a clever one." With a snap of his wrist, he brings the knife close to my face. "I'd take offense at that, being accused as a mason, but my friend here, his father was a bricklayer. Noble professions, both. But your man chose to *borrow* money rather than make it, and now it's time that he pay up."

My racing mind stutters over this new information. If they're not masons, they must be common moneylenders. My heart falls, thinking of my father's gold watch in John's pocket. Perhaps he meant to sell it to alleviate his debts. "If you're looking for money from John, it's too late," I say. "He's dead."

Confusion passes over my captor's face. "What are you on about? I don't need anything from any John. We're talking about Henry Campion. Your cousin."

I gape at him. Henry's world—the world of Walthingham Hall—could not seem further removed from these two.

"Do you hear me, girl? We need the full two thousand pounds. The odd painting and bits of jewelry aren't enough—and he'd better not try any more funny business, like setting that mutt on me. Your cousin's a cruel one, he is. Sending a little dog like that to do his dirty work. You think I wanted to break her neck?" He tests the knife on his thumb, his eyes set on some faraway point. "Now, *people*, they usually have it coming to them. You'll find I'm not averse to using the knife when it comes to them that deserve it."

As Tall moves closer to my face, I scratch at the hand clamped over my shoulder, but the big man pays me no more mind than if I were a stiff breeze. "I think I'll show you the value of the knife right now," his companion says conversationally. "How about this: We cut up your pretty face a bit, just to show your cousin we mean what we say?" He runs the tip of the thing along the curve of my lower lip. "I'm a dab hand with it, miss, and I promise you won't lose any more blood than I mean you to."

I drive the sharp toe of my boot into his shin as hard as I can. He doubles over in agony as I drive my head back into the big man's face. I hear the *thunk* of my skull connecting with his nose, and his grip on me loosens just enough. I make my body a dead weight, slipping through his arms onto the cobbled street.

I scrabble back to my feet, stagger a few steps, and then begin to run. Their shouts behind me quickly fade; I can only hope they are not so foolish as to pursue a well-dressed woman in ostentatious mourning garb through the streets of Bath. My skirts snatch at my legs, and my corset digs into my heaving ribs. But it feels good to run—I'd forgotten just how good. My feet know the way, even as my mind attempts to grasp what's just happened. Finally, I see the carriage, and I pound toward it, still imagining my captors just behind me, breathing at my neck. Matt's daydreaming in his seat, and his mouth falls open when he sees me.

"Lady Katherine!" he exclaims. Then, "Your hat!"

I bring my hand to my head—indeed, I've lost my hat in my headlong rush, and my hair is falling free. "Never mind it," I say, when I can speak again. "Just go on, get us out of here—take us back to Walthingham at once!"

My lip still tingles where the man traced it with the razor point of his knife. Collapsing back against the bench seat, I discreetly adjust my corset.

I have no doubt Tall would have sliced my face open without flinching. If he's capable of that, is he capable of murder? Perhaps it was he who came across my brother that day, painting white birches in the falling snow.

My mind spins as the horses dash down the road leading out of Bath. What financial mess has Henry involved himself in? And could his foolishness have caused my brother's murder?

The ride passes in a confused haze. I open the window to

let the cold air in, and my hair is whipped into a froth by the time we pull up in front of Walthingham. As I enter the house, I can think only of avoiding Henry and retiring to my room early. I've never needed to get my thoughts in order so badly as I do now.

My hand is on the door to my room when I hear a soft "Ahem" from behind me. Grace, dressed in a muted gray. I bite back the curse that comes to my lips.

"A word, Katherine?" she says, then turns and begins walking back down the hall. I have no choice but to follow her to her sitting room, done up smartly in ivory and blue, and altogether too many flounces and tassels for my taste. Tea is already steaming from a silver tray placed between two ottomans.

Her maid is nowhere in sight. As she deigns to serve me herself, I can tell she already knows about the proposal. A sense of bright expectation hums through her movements; even the decided way she raps her spoon against the slender side of her china cup speaks of the knowledge.

Finally, she hands across my tea and fixes me with a look. "No need to be coy with each other, Katherine. What are your intentions regarding my brother's proposal?"

The answer comes immediately to my lips. "I mean to refuse it," I say simply. "More than that, I'm returning to Virginia as soon as I can. I've already spoken to a lawyer."

The cup rattles against the saucer in her hand, but she regains her composure quickly, regarding me with shrewdness. "Mr. Simpson, I presume?"

I blush. "Indeed. He's been very helpful."

"Yes, I imagine he has. But, Katherine, won't you reconsider this rash act? You're needed here, at Walthingham. The estate is your birthright, the running of it your privilege. And Henry will make a very fine match for you. The estate's quarries are his, to add to your own inheritance, and he understands the workings of the house better than anyone."

If she only knew what I'd endured this afternoon, because of her "very fine" brother's actions, she might leave me alone. But, angry as I am, I can't burden her with it. Not until I understand the true extent of what Henry has done.

"Grace, I simply do not love him. And I never will." I hold up a hand, warding off her response. "Please believe that I know my own heart. I can never love him as a wife."

"I wasn't going to advise you on your heart, dear. Rather, I would remind you that marriage has little to do with hearts after the end of the first year. Adolescent infatuations are well and good, but building a marriage on naught but love is like building a house on sand."

There's a note of bitterness in her tone that makes me curious, but I don't push.

"Marriages are made by contract for a reason. The security and companionship of a match are all that can be expected by a reasonable woman of marriageable age."

"But I want more than that," I say softly. "Call me foolish if you must, but I want love in my life. I saw it between my parents, and I want it one day for myself."

"Your parents' illegitimate match is not a thing to emulate, Katherine," she says with sudden coldness. "Count yourself lucky to have been lifted from the circumstances their marriage confined you to, and do not set yourself up for the same kind of disaster."

I look at her squarely. "I've long suspected you felt that way,

Grace, but I'm sorry to hear you speak of my parents so harshly. You did not know my mother, so I will blame your words on your ignorance."

The icy silence that follows this is soon broken by a light knock at the door. Though I'm not surprised to see Henry standing in the doorway, the cold ripple of revulsion that runs through me in response takes me aback.

The smooth, handsome face, the elegant hands and manner of dress—they appear to me now as tools of deception, which he used to fool not just Jane but all of us. Who, seeing him, would dream him capable of such treachery?

I sit stiffly as he bestows a charming smile on us both. "Grace, might I speak to Katherine alone for a moment?"

Grace looks at me with barely concealed disgust and stands. "You may speak to her as long as you like, brother, for all the good it will do you. I'm glad to take my leave." She sweeps from the room, not bothering to look at me again.

Seeming untroubled by her words, Henry sits across from me, smiling in a way that I suppose is meant to look dashing. "I cannot wait any longer to speak with you, my love. Have you thought about my offer? Will you accept my suit?"

I respond in as steady a tone as I can muster. "I have considered your proposal, Henry, but I cannot accept. It will be impossible for us to marry, you see—I'm returning to America in a few days. There are matters to be settled first, of course, but my time here has caused me only pain. I just want to go home."

His smile falters during my speech but does not completely fade. "I understand your unhappiness, but we will make new memories together, beautiful ones. As man and wife, we will restore Walthingham Hall to its original greatness." He presses his hands into his knees, no longer looking at me. "You do not know the estate as I did, when I was a young man before the war. It was a magical place. We can lead a gilded life here, Katherine, together."

The fervor in his voice makes my skin crawl. "I thank you again for the compliment, but still I cannot marry you. We don't love each other, Henry, and Walthingham Hall is not my home. In fact, I mean to sell it."

Something passes behind his eyes then, in a flash—something ugly and hard. Just as quickly it's gone, and I see before me the rigidly controlled military man my cousin once was. "You mean to sell our home, Katherine?" he says tightly. "After all we've done for you? After all that we've given to you, taught you?"

Finally, my temper cannot be contained. "If the privileges of being Lady Katherine must come hand in hand with being restrained at the point of a knife, I'm not sorry to give it up," I say.

His eyes look stunned. "What are you talking about?"

"The men, the ones you owe money to. When they could not get hold of you, they found me instead. I know about your debts—though I don't care to know how you got them, thank you—and I was attacked because of them, because of you. What have you done, Henry? To what sort of people have you opened my home?"

He glares at me, his face an arrogant, remorseless mask. "Oh, but it isn't your home, Katherine. You said so yourself. You have always been an outsider here, unworthy to hold Walthingham Hall!"

"You are the unworthy one. Your thoughtless acts not only endangered my life, they cost me my only friend here." A sob escapes my throat. "How could you have been so cruel to Jane? You needn't ask, I'm sure, just why she's given me up."

For a long moment he doesn't respond, just regards me from below his lids with a look of brutal patience. Finally, he sighs. "You're young," he says heavily. "And you don't understand."

"I understand all too well. It's true, you have taught me much since I arrived in England—all about the hypocrisy and lies men are capable of. I think it's a lesson I will grow to value in time. But I repeat again, and for the final time: I cannot, I will not marry you."

"And you will sell Walthingham Hall?"

"I will. You and Grace will be provided for. Mr. Simpson will take care of it, I promise. But the house must be sold."

He stands slowly, his jaw tight and his face pale. "So be it, Lady Katherine. If that is as you wish it, that is how it will be."

I'm filled with a sense of dark triumph as his bowed figure limps from the room. Strange that, even as I prepare to sell the estate, I feel more like Lady Katherine than ever. I think of Mr. Simpson's warning—that I've changed, too much, perhaps, to return home. No, I decide. I'm still the same person I ever was. Henry's just now discovering that I'm more a Randolph than he'll ever be.

CHAPTER 21

I'M DREAMING OF blood-red leaves falling through the clear Virginia air. George is beside me, smiling up at them, glowing crimson in the fading sun. He stretches his fingers out to catch the warmth of it. I smile at him—and he turns suddenly toward me, catching my wrist tight in his fingers. His forehead, high and clear a moment before, now pulses with a livid gash, the same shade as the drifting leaves.

You're hurting me, I say, but he ignores me. As he moves his mouth to my ear, I smell the yawning, graveyard scent of his breath. *Go*, he whispers. *Run!*

And suddenly I'm awake in my bed, blinking against the blinding flare of a lantern. The hand curled cruelly around my wrist is not my brother's. As my eyes adjust, I see three figures standing over me.

Dr. Ebner, gripping my wrist; Henry, watching me with

hollow eyes; and a man I cannot name, who has a familiar face. "What's happening?" I croak, clutching the bedding to my chest with my free hand.

"It's for your own good," says Henry, his tone so cut through with malice that I recoil.

Then everything is happening far too quickly. Dr. Ebner pulls my arm straight out and behind me, the strange man does the same with the other, and they force me upright. In my shock I scream George's name; the doctor's grip slackens a moment, then returns with renewed strength. "Be quiet, girl. Would you prefer that we drug you?"

My arms are tied behind me with swift efficiency, the blankets stripped from my legs. They look pitifully bare and pale, the skirt of my nightgown riding up over them. After a pause, Dr. Ebner tugs the gown back down to my ankles.

Fighting to keep my head upright, I try to look them in the eyes. Some instinct makes me do it—I think it will make them recognize the monstrousness of what they're doing. But they won't look back at me.

Except for Henry. As the other men fight against me, tie my hands, he watches, his eyes trained on mine. To my horror, the doctor forces a band of thick, grimy-tasting fabric into my mouth, tying its ends behind my head. When I'm trussed, unable to scream, Henry steps forward and slaps me hard across the face.

Dr. Ebner looks away, uncomfortable, but says nothing. The other man only laughs. "She really is a wildcat, Henry, as you said. A pity she won't be your wife."

Between them they carry me into the hall, my struggles causing my limbs to chafe against the rough rope binding them. We pass Elsie, rubbing her eyes sleepily and holding a candle. "Lady Katherine?" she says in a tiny voice, then, eyes widening, she rushes forward. Holding her light in one hand like a ward, she clutches at Henry's hand on my thigh. He pushes her against the wall, and her candle clatters into darkness.

The men stink from their exertions, all sweat and smoke and sourness. A few servants have emerged from their quarters to see what's happening; when they catch sight of me, strung between the men, they avert their eyes and disappear back into the shadows of the hallway. Mrs. Whiting's eyes meet mine, and I think she'll say something, but she doesn't. My throat is raw from screaming around my gag, and my head sings with pain and confusion.

The last thing I see before I'm carried out the front door is Grace. She holds a lantern that illuminates the prim circle of her face. I can't speak, but try pleading for her aid with my gaze. She stares back at me coldly—as if she's never seen me before. It so chills my heart that for a moment I stop struggling.

Grunting, the men hoist me onto the bench of an unfamiliar carriage. I sit lopsided, my muscles screaming, as Dr. Ebner slips a black hood over my head. For a moment I go still. Catching sharp breaths through the rough fabric makes me so light-headed I nearly swoon.

"The hood quiets the patient, as you can see. Much like a horse in blinders." The cool, pedantic voice must be Dr. Ebner's, but the hood has the effect of flattening sound, and I can't be sure.

The man I cannot recognize is in higher spirits than the others, whooping and laughing as though this were just a moonlit lark. I hear him offering around a bottle of something that stinks sharper than whiskey. "She is a wildcat!" he keeps saying in satisfaction. But Henry's answering silence must wear him out, and soon the carriage rattling over the road is the only sound. Hunched on the seat in just my nightdress and bonds, I shiver and burn in turns, in the grip of a fever of fear and rage.

I wriggle my wrists in their ropes, but it seems only to make them tighter. Blind and mute, I find that I can't even squeeze out tears. For a time I try to keep track of our path, but fear disorients me and I soon give it up.

Then I start listening to the horses. Their hoofbeats are steady, and focusing on them makes my body stop shaking. After many, many minutes—an hour, at least—the carriage stops with a jerk.

"Heave ho," says the third man, his voice slurring as he pulls me upright and out of the carriage. I teeter like a drunk, cringing in the frigid air. Gravel digs into the soft undersides of my feet, and the hood is scraped from my face. We've halted on a patch of misty ground, beside wrought-iron gates furred with rust.

I blink in the half-light as the drunk man unties the ropes binding my feet and Dr. Ebner unlooses my gag. "You'll keep quiet now, won't you, Katherine? This will go better if you're calm." He smiles at me, almost kindly, then steps forward to the gates and sharply tugs the rope that hangs there. A bell rings harshly into the dim beyond.

I don't want to go through those gates. With everything that I am, everything that I know and can sense about this place, I do not want it. "Please," I say.

"What's that?" Henry is at my side, smelling strongly of liquor but perfectly upright, ever military in his bearing.

"Please," I say again. "Don't make me go in there."

His eyes are hard and bright, triumphant. "You're a willful girl, Katherine. Draw on that strength over these next weeks. Or years. You're going to need it."

Men's shapes appear in the gloom ahead of us, followed by the slight form of a woman. They open the gates, and, joining the three men who've brought me here, form a phalanx to usher me across the grounds.

The woman leads us, calling back to Henry as she walks. "She will be quite comfortable here, Mr. Campion," she says. "We appreciate your donation, and you needn't worry about your young cousin now that she's passed into our care."

It is then that I truly understand that Henry means to leave me here, friendless and lost. "This is mad!" I shout. "Where are you taking me? I haven't done anything wrong—I only refused to marry you!" For all the reaction I get, I might as well have remained silent.

"Dr. Ebner!" I try to get the old man to look at me. "You know this is wrong! Where have you taken me? What have I done to deserve punishment?" He looks straight ahead, trouble straining his brow.

Through the fog I see an imposing structure of dark-stained wood, looming nearly as large as Walthingham. Though ghostly lights flicker in some of the upper windows, the house keeps its secrets.

We pass through a pair of heavy wooden doors, thick as a fairy-tale castle's. Inside, the air smells of old dust and something sharp and medicinal. I stumble over a warped board in the near-dark. "Hello, Katherine," says the woman, finally looking at me. She's slender and stands as tall as a man. Her hair, scraped back from her spare face, is as black as mine.

"I am *Lady* Katherine," I say, shivering and ridiculous in my nightdress.

She turns fierce eyes toward Henry, then back on me. "I recommend you not overestimate your place in this world, girl. It will only lead to unhappiness. We don't value arrogance here, but peaceable tongues and docile manners. Remember that, and your lot won't be a miserable one. Mr. Cosley, take her to the third floor. There should be an open bed in the third cell."

"The third *cell*?" I cry. "Henry, where have you brought me? I tell you, I've done nothing wrong!" My voice trails off into a scream as a man with a thick mustache and meaty arms below rolled sleeves takes my two wrists in hand, squeezing them tight behind me. The strength in the gesture is enough to warn me that fighting against him will have no purpose.

As he marches me up the twisting stairs, I turn long enough to see Henry's face—a blank mask. Shuddering, I look away.

"Where am I?"

The man pays me no mind.

"My name is Lady Katherine Randolph," I try again. "And I am very rich."

A snort from him, and he yanks my wrists back, sending

a sharp sizzle of pain through my shoulders. I yelp without meaning to as we reach a threadbare landing.

A hallway lined in faded carpet stretches to either side of us, and the man veers left. To my horror, the doors we pass are bolted from the outside. *I know what kind of place this is.* I try to refuse the thought, but my sickness grows as we reach the third door, which he stops to unbolt. Then a dark cavity is yawning in front of me. Before I have time even to scream, my brutish escort shoves me on. I stumble into the room, and the door is bolted behind me.

I'm shocked to silence by the sudden blackness and the pungent stench of unwashed bodies that hits my nose with a slap. Slowly, my eyes adjust to the faint light coming from under the door. I can make out the shapes of three bunks arrayed against the walls in a U shape, and the faint wet glow of eyes watching me from the beds. Turning in fright, I bang my fists against the wood, calling out for help. I scream George's name; I scream Mr. Simpson's. When my skin begins to slip with blood, I start to kick.

Nobody comes, and the silence behind me is watchful and weary, all through my tantrum. Finally, a woman's voice comes from the nearest bunk. "Shut up, you. The bed beneath mine is empty, and you can consider yourself lucky for that. Lie down and stop your crying. Nobody's coming back for you tonight."

Her voice sounds calm in the darkness, a beacon of clarity. "What is this place?" I whimper, ashamed.

She laughs, the tone suddenly colored with dark humor. "You truly don't know? It's Temperley's House of Lunatics, stupid girl. Welcome home!"

CHAPTER 22

Despite the awful smell and the watery moaning and dry snores of the women around me, I try to sleep a little on my hard cot, wrapped in a blanket that does nothing to keep unseen bugs from biting my skin.

Between drifting into nightmares I cannot remember and waking to the real horror of my surroundings, my mind turns and turns. Why has Henry done this to me? Was it my refusal? The fact that I found out his secret? But why an asylum, of all places? I'm not mad, just grieving. Then I remember the day I found the bloody paintbrush, and the way my cousins looked at me as I raved. But still Henry professed to wanting my hand. He *knows* I am as sane as him. Saner.

When the answer comes to me, it's so obvious I could cry. I'm not mad, just fatally thoughtless: with George dead, I am the sole heir of Walthingham. And with me locked up, my sanity in question, *Henry* has become the Lord of Walthingham Hall—with all of the estate's vast wealth at his fingertips. No doubt he will summon his lawyers the moment the sun rises, to transfer over to him everything that was in my name.

Grace's face as I last saw it, stiff and uncaring, passes before my eyes. Did my cousins plot this together? My selling of the estate would have left them dependent on my charity, and on the small income of Henry's quarries. I was a fool to think they would not fight my decision and to underestimate the cruelties they're capable of. The Beast of Walthingham does exist, and there are two, beastly with greed and obsessed with maintaining a veneer of empty propriety.

My hands curl into fists as I think of Henry, cool and pressed, visiting the offices of Mr. Simpson's firm, sadly relaying the news of my mental breakdown.

It was inevitable, he'll say. *The loss of her parents, then her poor, dear brother—how much can a woman handle?*

But will Mr. Simpson believe me mad? My behavior at his lodgings was less than calm, but he could not have thought me truly broken. The memory of our closeness hits me with fresh pain. Why, oh, why did I pull away from his touch? I could so easily have fallen into his embrace, and now I may never see him again. It was pride, I think, or stubbornness. An unwillingness to take the easy route, to allow myself to be happy. Perhaps he was right. I *have* changed. I've let this place infect me, bind me with its strictures and rules, with its foolish clothes and modes of behavior. I wish, oh, I wish I had kissed him.

Or perhaps Henry will simply tell Mr. Simpson I'm gone,

on my way back to America without saying good-bye. Yes, it will be easier that way. Mr. Dowling will not think of me again, and even Jane will forget my imagined treachery. When I think of her warm sitting room, where I sat less than one day ago, I can hardly believe that such a place exists. My last thought before sleeping is a wish for a cup of Mr. Dowling's tea, hot in my palms and sweet with honey.

Waking in a cell is harder than waking the morning after George's death. The room does not improve by daylight, what little of it manages to trickle through the window. The five women turning in their beds are of various ages, each clothed in a dress of plain gray. The walls of our prison are papered over in peeling blue-and-white stripes, like something an Englishwoman might choose for the walls of her child's nursery. Of the five women sharing the room, three still lie quiet under blankets no nicer than mine. A woman of about forty rocks back and forth in her bed; it takes me long minutes to realize that the airless hiss I'm hearing is a stream of whispered words issuing from her lips, without meaning or pause. An older woman with a stony face stands next to a curtain, behind which is the room's single convenience. She does not speak or smile, but raps the wall beside her with her fist in an endless cadence that I think will drive me mad, until she stops and retreats behind the curtain. The smell that fills the room soon after is worse than the tapping, and I bury my face in my hands, finally allowing myself to cry.

The bed overhead creaks, and the woman I spoke to last night drops her head over the edge, watching me through a curtain of lank, whitish hair. "I'm Margaret," she says. "I met you."

"Yes," I choke, swiping at my damp eyes. Even now, I'm unwilling to let strangers see me sob. "And you told me this place was a madhouse. I don't belong here—I'm not mad in the least; I've been betrayed."

Her eyes go wide with concern. She disappears for a moment, and then climbs down to sit beside me. "Tell me what's been done to you, poor child," she says in a soothing voice. My heart leaps in hope as I tell her of my predicament, from Henry's proposal at Walthingham Hall to my late-night transport to this horrible place. She nods in recognition as I speak, her eyes growing bright.

Her voice is sad when she replies. "Your story is much like mine. You see"—she looks about, as if to see who is listening to us—"I, too, have been locked up because of a great injustice."

I grab her hand impulsively. "Did your husband send you away?"

She shakes her head. "Not my husband, my father. I was never allowed to marry—were I to have children, I would become even more dangerous to my enemies."

"Your enemies?" I ask, my neck prickling.

She nods. "I have a great many. You see, I am the illegitimate daughter of the king!"

I gape at her, unsure whether to laugh or to cry. The wretched woman is at least as old as King George himself.

"Nobody believes your lies, you old fool," says a voice from across the room, raw and low. "You're no more a princess than I am the Pope."

Margaret jerks to her feet. "And you're a rotten trollop!" she snarls, her eyes wet and wild.

The girl who spoke is lying on the top bunk just across from us, and she swings her legs down and jumps to the floor, her dark eyes trained on Margaret. "What am I, now?"

The old woman whimpers, scurrying back to her bunk. The girl ignores her and turns her gaze on me. I try not to squirm beneath its intensity.

"Did I hear you right?" she asks. "Did you say you come from Walthingham?"

"Yes, I did. I am the heir of Walthingham Hall."

She rushes to my side and kneels before me. Her teeth are browned, her skin dull, but I can see that she might once have been pretty. "Have you seen my baby?" she asks.

"Your baby?" I repeat dumbly.

"My child, my baby! Have you seen her? A sweet little thing, she'd be. Not yet two. Eyes dark, like mine. Please, have you seen her?"

She's snaked her fingers around my upper arm, digging her nails into tender skin. "Stop!" I hiss. "I don't know who you are or what you're talking about. Get off me!"

The girl slaps me, not hard. Her voice is quieter now, desperate. "Quiet, or you'll bring them. I don't mean you any harm; just answer my question and I'll let you alone. Have you seen my child?"

I hear the clatter of feet from the hall, then the bolt on the door is thrown back with a hollow *clang*. Mr. Cosley and another man, both in shirtsleeves, hurry in. The girl pays them no mind, gripping me harder. "Just tell me if she lives," she whispers. "Too many nights, I fear she does not. I only saw her the once, just for a minute. . . ."

I scratch at her fingers, managing to pry one hand away as the guards close in. "I tell you, I don't know!" I cry.

"This one again," says Cosley disgustedly. He and the other men drag her back as easily as if she were a stuffed doll. "She needs more letting. We've neglected this too long—the bad blood is showing itself."

The worst part is not the way she does not fight as they pull her to her feet. The worst part is the sudden vacancy in her eyes, as if all that she is, all that she thinks, has retreated to a space deep inside her, leaving her body a pliant shell.

I throw out a hand before the men can lead her away. "Sirs, wait. I need to see whoever is in charge. There's been a mistake—I'm not meant to be here. I'm not meant to be here!"

The men smirk at me as I plead. "You'll get your turn with the man in charge," Mr. Cosley sneers. "Eventually."

CHAPTER 23

An hour or so after the woman is taken away, I hear the sound of doors being unbarred all along the hall. I can't stop staring at our door, longing for even the finite freedom beyond—anything that will take me from the stench of this terrible room. Finally we, too, are let free and led downstairs to a dingy dining hall: two long plank tables flanked by rough-hewn benches, with a single window set high in the white-washed wall. I gaze hungrily at the square of sky I can see beyond it, longing for the sight of a bird, a frill of cloud, any proof that life beyond this place is not a dream.

There are around thirty of us, all women, everyone but me in matching gray. The oldest among us is bent and pale, and the youngest younger than me. As she shifts in her seat, moving a hand to her back, I see with a start the telling swell of stomach beneath her dress. I've heard of girls in trouble being sent away, but I could not have conceived of them being sent to a place like this. It's no place for a mother, much less a child.

When a bowl is set down before me, I find I cannot eat. Though the women around me set to with a kind of desperate gusto, the grayish porridge in my bowl looks nothing like any food I've ever eaten.

The woman serving us, a sturdy figure in dowdy blue, sees me pick up my spoon, then discard it without managing a bite of gruel. "The food's not good enough for the little lady?" she says.

"Calling this 'food' is an act of great imagination," I reply.

The woman's eyes flash as she charges toward me, her arms flexing below the thin cotton of her work dress. She grabs my hand before I can snatch it away, and wraps my fingers around the spoon, crushing them into the metal.

"There, now, Your Highness. Eat and be grateful." Her breath is sharp in my nose as she bends my unyielding hand toward the bowl. "And don't go thinking you'll always get the royal treatment."

"Thank you, Mrs. Withers; that will be enough. The master wants to speak to this one." The woman I met last night stands in the doorway, her coloring even more severe by daylight.

Mrs. Withers steps back, letting my hand drop. "She won't get to eat again till supper," she says grudgingly. "But why that should be my concern, I don't know."

"It isn't, and it won't be. Miss Randolph, follow me at once. You're to speak with Mr. Temperley."

I stand up quickly, trying to look confident and very, very sane, but I'm still wearing the nightdress I went to bed in. It seems days ago that I put it on, in my warm, firelit room at Walthingham Hall, and the starched white cotton has grown limp and grimy in the hours since.

The woman leads me through austere white halls, badly lit, to a room with its door half-open. "I see you there," a man calls. "Bring in the patient, please."

The room we enter is colder than the rest of the house, with a large picture window overlooking the wild patch of land this place clings to. I drink in the watery light until Mr. Temperley turns, and his odd appearance distracts me completely.

Long, straight furrows run along either side of his mouth, cut clean and deep as if into stone, and three more lines score his high forehead, under a crop of hair the color of old ivory. His eyes, while not cruel, have a look of indifferent vacancy that gives me little hope.

"Thank you, Mrs. Temperley. You may leave us now," he says briefly, his eyes raking over me. Is that woman his wife, then? Or his sister-in-law? He watches her go, then folds himself into the chair behind his great, dark-wood desk. There is nowhere else to sit in the room, so I continue standing.

"I'm told you are a troublemaker," he says without inflection.

I sputter a moment before regaining my poise. "No, I couldn't be. I mean, I'm not. I only got here last night, and I haven't done anything. But, sir, I'm really not meant to be here at all."

"I, I, I. The earmarks of a common narcissist, at the least." He pulls a ledger from atop a teetering stack of books, and makes a notation that I cannot see. Then he looks back up at me, still without expression. "All over England—all over the world, I imagine—there are hospitals like mine, populated solely by those who believe they 'aren't meant to be here.' Your opinion on the matter holds little weight, Lady Katherine."

I don't trust his use of my title—it seems designed to placate me. "My opinion is the only one that can be valid, sir. I stand before you, sane. I will submit to any level of questioning to prove my point. I ask only that you allow me to leave this place at once, and send for a carriage for my transport."

His fair eyebrows rise so high they nearly disappear into his yellowing hair. "And just how does a young woman, sound of mind and body, get herself committed to a rest facility such as this one?"

I take a deep breath and look into his eyes, attempting to keep my voice steady and strong. "I believe I was placed here at the behest of my cousin Henry Campion, who wishes to gain control of my estate. When I would not marry him, he took this more expedient path toward my fortune. He needs it to pay off his debts, which I learned about when the men he borrowed from accosted me in Bath. Not only this, but my brother was recently . . ." I trail off, feeling I may have said too much. "Recently deceased," I finish lamely.

Mr. Temperley has steepled his long hands together and watches me raptly over discolored fingertips. "Fascinating," he says. "Your hysterical behavior should have been recognized much earlier than this. As it is, your lunatic fantasies are more fully developed than any I've encountered. It is a good thing, Lady Katherine, that you've found your way into my care. We will make great strides toward your recovery, I'm sure."

"Blast it," I cry, slamming my palms down on his desk. "Everything I've told you is true. My cousin is the insane one—insane with greed. You'll be committing a crime, holding a healthy person here against her will."

"You might want to brush up on the finer points of law, my lady," he says, rummaging through his desk. "And this is all the proof I need of your regrettable illness: its confirmation by two of my most respected colleagues in the medical profession."

The piece of paper he slaps onto the desk reads *Certificate of Insanity* in plain script. Below it are scrawled the name of the traitorous Dr. Ebner, and the corroborating signature of a man whose name is familiar to me: Lieutenant Reginald Hastings. At last, it clicks into place: The third man, the stranger who helped Henry and Dr. Ebner drag me from my bed, was also my first dancing partner the night of the ball.

I want to scream this new bit of proof into Mr. Temperley's face, but it will only strengthen his opinion of me as a seeker of conspiracies. I keep my voice low. "Sir, the two names here belong to intimates of Henry: his family doctor, his fellow serviceman. This is nothing but proof that I have not been properly examined by a doctor unconnected with my cousin's terrible plan."

"Your cousin served our country in the war. He is a

serviceman and a hero. The lieutenant, also a hero and an upstanding young medical professional. And Dr. Ebner, why, he treated my own fevers when I was a younger man. Am I to question the opinions of these men in favor of the fantastic claims of a sixteen-year-old girl, far from home and clearly grieving the untimely loss of a sibling?

"I tell you again, and this is my final word on the matter: Your stay here will be valuable to us both. In a few months' time, your treatment may well have resolved the worst of your issues, but that remains to be seen. . . ."

"A few months?" I cry. "I need to leave this awful place at once!"

"You know that is impossible," he says with dry patience. "I'm only speaking to you now as a courtesy to your family; really, patients respond best when they are left *out* of the conversation as regards their treatment."

"May I have writing paper, at least, so that I might post a letter? My family will wonder what's become of me." I think of my foster parents, and of Mr. Simpson.

His brow furrows even more deeply as he frowns at me. "I don't think you quite understand your situation here. You are to be kept, as all our patients are, in isolation from your usual situation of life. We find that is most conducive to our patients' mental rehabilitation. And now I believe I have indulged your questioning long enough. It is my hope that we do *not* meet again soon, as the treatments I supervise are generally needed only for our more recalcitrant patients. . . ."

I stand silent a moment, letting him speak, while retracing in my mind's eye the path I took to get to his office. I think I can find the front door from here. I tilt my head slightly to the right and see that the door behind me stands ajar. Before I can overthink it, I push a teetering stack of books forward onto Temperley and dart toward the door. He shouts with surprise as I pound out of the office and down the hall. I dodge what looks like a wandering patient, a woman in gray who claps happily as I pass her. When I glimpse the front door at the end of a creaking corridor, my heart leaps. I run toward it, my fingers grasping forward.

"Got her!" says a voice behind me as a thick arm loops around my waist and yanks me off my feet. I struggle against the corded muscle binding me, my feet kicking uselessly at the air.

After a moment Mr. Temperley appears at the other end of the hall, walking with exaggerated slowness and holding a bundle of gray fabric in his hand. "Release her," Temperley says tonelessly, pushing the gray thing toward me. The guard lets me go, and I spend a moment catching my breath.

"You are not Lady Katherine now," says Temperley in a measured cadence. "Here there is no hierarchy, no difference in station. You are a patient like any other. And your attempts to cause trouble will not be tolerated."

I throw the dress back at him in disgust. "I won't wear this."

A slight sneer curls his lip. "You can put it on yourself, or my men can assist you. Which would you prefer?"

The guard's smile at this raises the hair on my neck. After a moment, I stoop to pick up the garment. I'm allowed the use of an anteroom cluttered with boots and jackets to change. I imagine myself attacking Mr. Temperley with the heavy heel of a man's boot, but the thought is fleeting and without spirit.

Though I've been longing to peel off my now-filthy nightgown, I feel sickened by the constricting gray cloth. It makes me feel, for the first time, as if I might really belong here.

When I reenter the hall, clad in scratchy gray, a guard whisks the nightgown from my hands. I'm given a shapeless cloak and a pair of soft-soled shoes—the kind that would offer no resistance against rough ground, were I to escape somehow—and ushered into a high-walled courtyard.

The rest of the women, wrapped in cloaks like mine, are gathered in the muted daylight. The walls are crawling with the husks of old ivy, and stone benches sit beside urns slimy with moss. I see a guard at the garden's edge talking to a bright-haired inmate, who is laughing at something he's saying. She's pretty until you look too closely at her eyes. The pregnant girl I saw at breakfast sits beside a slightly older companion, who puts her arm around the younger girl with an air of protective ownership. But most of the patients sit or stand alone. One, crouching, crumples dead leaves and lets the fragments slip through her fingers.

I feel exposed under the open sky. It's maddening to be outside yet still so trapped.

Margaret sidles up beside me, poking a bony finger into my arm. "Duchess Katherine," she says. "I've heard wonderful news from court." Her breath smells like sour mash. Though I jerk my face away from hers, she keeps talking. "My father has accepted me at last—I'm going to London in a gilded carriage this very night!"

She flutters her arms out and does a spin, closing her old eyes against the sun. I look from face to muttering face, then down at my own gray dress, and the horror of my new life threatens to pull me completely under. Beyond caring, beyond pride, I run to the garden wall, beating my scabbed fists against it and falling to my knees. Before the indifferent eyes of thirty broken women, I weep.

CHAPTER 24

After a time, I'm pulled roughly to my feet.

"That's enough of that, now. You're setting off the other ones," the guard says. He points his chin toward a sobbing woman, her unfocused eyes trained loosely on me. I swipe at my streaming eyes, and he retreats back to his bench, pulling out a tin of tobacco and shoving a plug into his mouth. As I survey the yard, my eyes fall on a second-story window. Mrs. Temperley is looking down at me, and for a moment my eyes meet hers.

Steel comes into my spine, and for a moment I feel myself again. The guard is right. That's enough of that. It was foolish of me to try running this morning, and I should not have let myself break down in front of everyone.

But there must be a way out of here. I scan the tops of the walls, vowing that I won't draw attention to myself again. Even in these shoes, even in this dress, I could run far and fast away from here, if I could just get over these walls. They're steep, impossible to climb, but there will be other doors and windows. All I need to do is learn the routines of this place and find a weakness. I think of the raccoons back at the ranch—the way they scampered over the roof waiting for a moment when the door was open and they could pillage our stores. We learned not to underestimate them, but still they'd catch us out from time to time. And sometimes it wasn't even clear how they managed it. If a raccoon could find a way, then so can I.

I look at the women around me, bedraggled gray birds, and wonder how many were truly mad when they came to this place—and how many were driven to madness by unfair imprisonment and by the Temperleys' "treatments." I try to judge whether any of them could prove an ally. The pregnant girl's companion gives me a hard, fierce look, but the others avoid eye contact. I notice that the bright-haired girl and the guard have disappeared, and dig my nails into my palm to keep myself from speculating where. No, there won't be any help from these poor souls, I think. They've been here too long, and their hopes have been ground to dust.

Just then, the wild woman from the morning, my cell mate, is escorted into the yard. Her sleeve is rolled up, revealing a new white bandage just below her elbow. She walks with the tentative, searching steps of a person with seasickness. Her eyes scan the yard, finally resting on me.

I stiffen as she approaches, her face looking resolute and quite sane. She stops a little way away from me and puts up her palms. "I'm begging your pardon, miss. I know that I frightened you today. Please, may I sit beside you?" When I nod my head slightly, she feels her way toward a bench and sits. "I couldn't help myself. Hearing the name of Walthingham . . . it puts bad things into my mind." For a moment she pulls at her dark hair fiercely, as if to ease the hot anger in her head.

"Tell me what happened to you at Walthingham," I say quietly, not wishing to upset her, or to bring the attention of the guards. Perhaps I can gain some helpful information from this woman, in time.

"You came from there, didn't you? Is it true, what they said—that you're the heir of Walthingham Hall?"

"It is."

"My name is Dorothy—perhaps you knew my sister there. She would be seventeen now. Her name is Elsie. She was on her way to being a lady's maid when I left. . . ." Her voice is touched with desperation, and she tugs again at her hair. The pain of it seems to calm her.

"Elsie was my dressing maid!" Just saying her name brings unexpected lightness to my heart. "She said she had a sister once—does she know that you're here? The way she spoke, I thought that you had died."

"They likely told her I was dead, and I might as well be," she says starkly. "I wish I had died, rather than have my child taken away."

"Who took your child?" I breathe. "What happened?"

She starts speaking fast, in a near monotone, and I crane my head toward hers to hear. "I was the lady's maid to Grace Campion when I got pregnant. I hid it. For a very long time, I hid it. Elsie knew, of course—we let out my dresses together. She helped me with my duties when I was struggling. My poor little sister, she barely slept that last month. I was often ill from the child, always cross with Elsie. I regret it now. I wish that our last weeks together had been happy ones.

"The baby came early, before I was discovered. I gave birth to her in a china cupboard. Such a little thing! And eager to come, too. She came out squalling, smart as can be." A smile touched her face then was gone, like a flash of blue weather.

"But there was no hiding it then, of course. I thought Miss Campion would make me go that very day, but she didn't. She hid her feelings well; I know that now." My heart climbs into my throat, waiting to hear of Grace's treachery.

Dorothy continues, still looking down. "She told me another woman would watch after my child, someone with a wet nurse. I didn't believe that anyone rich enough to have a wet nurse would want an unmarried maid's child, but she promised me they would." She looks shyly up at me. "I named her Violet. Just for myself—nobody else ever heard the name. I never even got to nurse her."

"I'm sorry," I whisper.

She shrugs. "I cried for days, though I still did my work like before. I just cried when nobody could hear me, and a lot at night. Elsie tried to help me, but the sadness felt like quicksand. I couldn't pull myself free of it. Finally, Miss Campion told me I could visit my child. When she said that, I fell to my knees in front of her. I kissed her hand, so grateful. It makes me sick to think of it now. She rode with me in the carriage, right through the gates of this horrible place. I knew right away that something was wrong—two men had to pull me from the carriage, screaming. Miss Campion just looked at me like I was already invisible, like I was already dead. I've wished I was, every day since. I've grown old in this place, waiting for it."

She falls silent, her hands kneading the ragged ends of her hair. Grace's face the day of the hunt, half in sun and half in shade, comes back to me. And her words: *Though it was never proven, the baby Elsie's sister carried was believed by many of the servants to be John's.*

"The baby's father," I say. "Did he try to find you?"

She looks at me, uncomprehending. "Try to find me? He's the one who had me sent away."

"B-but," I say. "How could a footman have you sent away?"

"A footman?"

"John," I say. "He's still . . . he was still at Walthingham."

She laughs, a small and bitter sound. "That young pup? No, it wasn't him. The father was Lord Walthingham's nephew. Henry Campion."

After a stunned moment, I laugh. A real laugh, at my own small-mindedness, my cursed lack of imagination. How can I continually be shocked by the cruel hypocrisy my cousin has again and again proven himself capable of? So this is where he disposes of any who encumber him. I look across the yard, and my stomach sinks. I wonder how many others here are his victims, or victims of men like him.

"My cousin," I say. "He's the one who has imprisoned me here. Are you not surprised?" I laugh again, loud enough to draw the attention of Margaret, who has been sitting in a regal pose on a nearby bench, no doubt preparing herself for the imminent attentions of the king.

"He would've married me if he could," I tell her. "But only after he ruined my friend, the girl he'd promised himself to.

Perhaps he'll marry her still, now that he has my fortune in his hands." I'm frightened at the hysterical pitch of my voice. A quick glance around assures me that it's gone unnoticed. "I underestimated him," I whisper to Dorothy, who watches me with wide eyes. "But I will not make that mistake again."

CHAPTER 25

EVEN IN OUR windowless cell, we can hear the storm. It makes the other women restless—I hear Margaret above me, whimpering in her sleep—but it makes me feel less alone. The rage I've kept tamped tight for the past five days seems to find its vent in the whipping wind. It whistles in through hidden crevices and freshens the fetid air.

Less welcome is the dampness. The rains began the day before yesterday, and they haven't let up. Instead of forcing us to take our rest in the sodden yard, the guards make us sit at meals for an extra hour, before sending the healthiest among us to work. Yesterday I dipped stained sheets in and out of huge vats of soapy gray water, squeezing them dry until my hands could no longer hold a fist. Mrs. Temperley oversees the laundry, her great raw knuckles standing out as she twists her hands together and issues brusque orders. She is far younger than Mr. Temperley, but I've learned that they're not siblings but married. It's rumored that she was a patient once, but I don't put much stock into what the others tell me.

My hopes at finding a weakness in the guards' routine has been disappointed. All the windows I have seen in the patients' areas are reinforced with bars. As far as I can tell, there are only three ways into the secure areas of the building: the front door; the gate that leads to the exercise yard; and there must be a back door, where deliveries of coal and food are made, though I haven't seen it. That passage offers the only chance of escape that I can see, but I would bet the door leading to the staff area is always locked and each of the guards carries a key. I have little faith in my pickpocketing skills. If I am to obtain a key, I fear it will have to be through violence.

Though we're kept under guard, we find ways to communicate. Even in this terrible company, alliances are quickly formed. I have five roommates, including Margaret and Dorothy. One is a German woman named Ilse, who does not speak, but passes her time in a haze of strange compulsions: moans, rhythmic rapping. She's the maddest among us. Elizabeth is the protective companion of the pregnant girl. She's strongly built and the daughter of a prominent barrister; I think she's here because she refused to marry. I feel sorriest for Anne, a woman of at least sixty who looks perpetually confused. She was placed here by her son, and though she won't speak against him, I think his motives were like Henry's: based in greed. Anne prays often, her fingers reaching to the place at her neck where I'm sure a cross once hung. We're not allowed any ornament here. Her fingers grasp empty air.

None of us sleeps through the night, it seems, and barely

an hour goes by that my sleep isn't broken by nightmare cries from another bunk, or by a woman's rush to the chamber pot. But I haven't complained since that first day in the yard. I eat their food when it is served to me, I suffer the indignity of the shared privy, and I do not act as though I think it's all below me. Since the day I broke down in the yard, I have been a model inmate.

It's so easy, easier than I ever would have imagined, to lose yourself in a place like this. My hands are the hands of a madwoman already—roughened by harsh soap, scabbed over from the night I pounded on the doors of our cell. My hair is a madwoman's hair, so ratted up in back that it will not lie flat past the neck of my dress. Though we're allowed to wash, they don't give us anything for it but a stinking cake of black soap. The sickest among us have their hair shorn short and bristling. They're the ones with haunted eyes, the ones whose blood is let so often it's a wonder that the veins showing under their papery skin still hold color.

I struggle to comb out my hair with my fingers, and pray they will not see fit to cut it off. Though I make my face blank, thoughts of Henry animate my waking hours and dog my sleep. He must have been planning all along to get his hands on Walthingham. My fears of harmless old McAllister, the foolish fancies of a beast stalking the woods—all distractions from the stark truth of my cousin's greed. I can expect no help from outside this place. Mr. Simpson must believe that I'm on my way to America; Jane never wants to see me again. And Grace, who might have saved me, simply turned her face away.

But I can still help myself. And tonight, I've finally

managed to pry loose one of the wooden slats beneath my pitifully thin mattress. My fingertips are rough with splinters, but the feel of the sturdy wood in my palm calms me.

I look across the room and catch the flash of Dorothy's open eyes. Though we haven't had the privacy of the yard, we've still taken advantage of every moment we found ourselves unwatched. She's told me all she can about how this place is run. I know that there are four guards on duty at all times, and that they change shifts twice a day, at the peal of a bell. I know that the two silent maids in drab caps are not our allies, that they've informed on past patients who have been foolish enough to beg them for aid. I know that the windows are all barred, with the exception of the one in Mr. Temperley's office.

And I know that the only time we're not watched is when we're locked into our dorms at night. The weapon in my hand is proof of that one small privacy.

Dorothy is still looking at me from across the room, and I give her a sharp nod. At my signal, she gets up from her bed, then drops onto the middle of the floor, moaning.

Quickly I move to the grille of the door and put my mouth to it.

"Please come, quick! One of the women is ill!" My voice sounds tenuous, unused. I've barely spoken above a whisper for days.

After a long moment, a pane of light appears on the wall outside, as from an unseen door being thrown open. Within it I see a guard's unresponsive shadow.

"Hurry, please!" I repeat. "She's not well!"

I'm sure the guards have been playing cards and making

themselves slow with liquor, and my heart leaps with sudden hope. *This might work.*

"What's this racket about?" a man calls. Mr. Umberland. Just so long as it isn't Cosley, who can smell a lie from a mile away.

"A girl is sick; come quickly."

"Unless the girl is dying, I don't want to hear nothing from you after the lights are put out." The door starts to close again, and I cry out frantically.

"No, please, don't leave us alone! Help us, help us!"

The women in my cell are awake now and grumbling, watching Dorothy on the floor, and I hear a woman in the next cell over mocking me. *"Help us, help us,* she says. Stupid girl."

Perhaps sensing the beginnings of a small mutiny, the guard sighs and clips heavily toward our cell.

"This had better be good. I'm in half a guinea to Smith." As he unlocks the door, I flatten my body against the wall just beside it. Before he can move entirely into the room, I squeeze my eyes shut and bring the bed slat down over his head. It connects with a *thump* that rings through my fingers.

He looks at me, shocked, then falls to one knee with a groan. Praying I don't kill him, I bring the thing down over his head one more time as Dorothy jumps to her feet, staring. The man lies still now, and to their everlasting credit, the women in our cell say not a word, simply staring at the felled guard.

"Stop gaping and move!" I hiss at Dorothy. The door to the guards' room is closed, but I know it can't remain so for long. I slip the ring of keys from beneath the guard's heavy body and rush from the room, Dorothy at my heels. Silently, I shut the door behind us and bolt it.

We move through the corridors as if in a dream, our feet fleet and silent, every step perfectly placed, and I think to myself again, *This could work; we've very nearly done it.* My heart beats so loudly that Temperley himself must hear it, and my neck is cold with sweat. But we're not followed, the other women don't give us away, and no lights turn on in our wake.

Down the stairs, through the hallway, and finally to the front door. It seems to pulse in the dark, with its promise of escape.

Dorothy dawdles a bit as we reach it, and I grab her arm to pull her along. With a stab of pity, I remember that she has not left this place in almost three years. "It's all right," I whisper as I scramble through the keys. "I won't leave your side."

Miraculously, the front door unlocks with the second key I try. Then it opens, and I can smell the fresh air beyond. . . .

But a bell starts to ring, high and frantic, clearly meant to alert Mr. Temperley to fugitives. With no time to rue my foolishness, I run, yanking Dorothy into motion beside me.

We flee over soggy ground, wisps of fog lapping at our ankles. There's a shout from behind, but we're moving too quickly to hear it clearly. I duck my head against the rain, and the gate looms up so suddenly I can barely stop myself in time.

"Climb!" I scream, gripping the freezing metal slats in my fists. The metal is rough through my thin slippers, but I start climbing steadily. I'm nearly at the top when Dorothy cries out, a long sound as the breath is knocked out of her.

She's lying on her back at the foot of the gates, looking

stunned from the fall. I hesitate for one long moment, and then climb down beside her.

"Get up, get up!" I cry frantically. "Can your legs still work?" She turns her face away, wincing miserably. She's given up.

And by then it's too late. A guard in a flapping coat is bearing down on us. I see the short club in his hand before I feel it: one quick rap at my ribs, and the pain drops me to my knees in the mud. I try to block Dorothy's body with my own, but no more blows come. The guard is looking away from us, back toward the house.

A wavering lantern beams thinly through the rain. I smear the water from my face, panting against the sharp pain in my chest. Soon Mr. Temperley comes into view, his lantern casting deep shadows over his furrowed face. Though it's the middle of the night, he's fully dressed and moves without hurry.

"Did I not warn you?" He speaks low, but I hear him clearly. "I told you to behave, lest we need to put you on a more trying regimen."

Dorothy cringes away, hiding her face in her hands, and an abyss of guilt opens up beneath me. She wasn't ready for this. Of *course* she wasn't ready for this.

Temperley snaps his fingers. "Get up, both of you. And you," he addresses the guard, "ready the cells for solitary confinement."

At those words my mind goes blank, and I scramble onto my knees, as if I can try one more time for freedom. This is clearly what Mr. Temperley has been waiting for. "The strait-jacket," he says grimly.

As Dorothy lies hopeless on the ground, the two men bring

me to my feet, and the guard produces a white jacket from inside his coat. They wrap me tightly, pinning my arms uselessly to my chest. Though I know struggling will only make it worse, I can't stop screaming. My breath rasps against the place in my chest where I was hit.

"Tomorrow, your new treatment will begin." Temperley's face is so close to mine that I cannot miss the sadistic gleam below his usual impassiveness. "Bloodletting and emesis will be required to bring you into order. But do not despair, child. You may one day be fit to return to society—once your waywardness has been purged."

CHAPTER 26

M Y EYES ARE barely open when the guard's upon me, pulling me to my feet. The blank mercy of dreamless sleep is quickly overtaken by the reality of my tiny cell, the stink of stale urine, the ache in my chest. I feel a sick scraping when I breathe too deeply, and wonder if something inside of me has been broken.

My body keeps fighting by instinct, though the guard only laughs at my feeble struggles. We pass another barred cell some yards down a skinny corridor, where Dorothy still lies asleep. Silently, I wish her many hours of uninterrupted slumber.

I'm dragged up a short flight of stairs to a flat trapdoor in the ceiling. We emerge, blinking, into a windowless, white-walled room. An ominous stain stretches across the wooden floor, nearly reaching my feet in their sodden slippers. But I'm more frightened by the table at the room's center: long, flat, bristling with leather restraints. The guard lifts me onto it with no more trouble than he'd have had with a baby.

My mind flashes back to George, lying on his cold table in the west wing. It seems impossible that there ever existed a person who loved me as much as he did, who could protect me from the world.

"There, you've shut up a minute," the guard is saying, securing the bonds around my feet. "Clever of you. It'll go easiest that way."

When the door swings open, I can see enough clean white light to guess that it's at least midday. A man enters the room wearing a slightly overlarge dark suit. The lamplight beams dully off his large signet ring, and in his hands he holds a tray. On it lie white bandages, a scalpel, and a length of tube.

"Where is Mr. Temperley?" I say, my voice spiking with panic.

"Keep your voice down, Miss Randolph," the man says in blandly soothing tones. "This process will be far more comfortable if you don't struggle." He nods, and the guard leaves the room.

I watch him go, tasting acid at the back of my throat. "Please, let me speak to him. I'll be good. You don't need that scalpel; he'll tell you. Please . . ."

"Mr. Temperley is gone for the day, tending to business in Bath. And besides, he's the one who prescribed your treatment."

He cuts methodically through the stays of the straitjacket, until my left arm can be pulled free. It looks small and pale, like it belongs to someone I do not know. The pitiful limb is pulled straight and belted to the table.

The man's fingers run over the tube, the bandages. They settle with a featherweight touch on the shining scalpel. As he lifts it, I bring my eyes back to the white expanse of my arm, its unbroken skin. Then I squeeze my eyes shut and pray.

There's a knock at the door. My eyes snap open and fly to the man's impatient face. He seems to weigh his options a moment before sighing and replacing the scalpel gently on the tray.

He opens the door partway. "What is it, Mr. Cosley?" His voice is sharp.

"The girl has a visitor. Waiting now in Mr. Temperley's study."

The doctor huffs loudly. "Can it not wait? I have very specific instructions."

"He's some kind of legal fellow—perhaps best if we leave the girl in one piece, at least until he's seen her." Cosley laughs as the doctor casts an indifferent look back at me.

"Yes, I suppose so. Make her presentable first."

I'm flooded with dumb, animal relief, so that I can barely stand. The two men untie me, drag me to my feet, pull the jacket off the rest of the way. A clean gray dress is found and given to me. After they turn their backs, I slide it over my skin, so sensitive with fear that it tingles as if slapped.

I'm praying that it's Mr. Simpson. I can think of no one else. The two men flank me on the silent walk toward Temperley's office. And when I see his face, brooding in the underlit anteroom, my heart swells with painful gladness. I break from Cosley's light grip and run straight into William's arms.

He allows me to hold him a moment, before detaching

himself and stepping back. "Good afternoon, Lady Katherine," he says with careful politeness. His eyes on mine bring me back to myself.

"Good afternoon, Mr. Simpson." My dirty fingernails are fisted into my palms, out of sight. Mr. Simpson silently takes in my ratted hair, my shock-white skin, before putting a firm hand out to the doctor.

"Thank you for harboring Lady Katherine in this difficult time. My clients and I take great comfort in knowing that she was given proper treatment and rest. But now I must get her home to Walthingham."

"I had no such information from Mr. Temperley," the doctor says suspiciously. "The girl will stay here until we're given express orders otherwise by him."

Mr. Simpson draws himself up. His eyes grow bored and his jaw juts. "Sir, I am the solicitor acting on behalf of the Walthingham estate. Understand that I have the full authority of Walthingham at my back, and am therefore authorized to remove Lady Katherine from your care at any time." With a sharp snap he opens his flat leather case, removing a piece of paper from within. He passes the thing beneath the doctor's skeptical eyes, and I hold my breath. I feel if I try to lend my voice to his, it will do no good.

The doctor's tone is more conciliatory now. "All the same, I prefer that we wait until the Temperleys return. It won't be long now, Mr. . . . . ?"

Mr. Simpson returns his cool gaze. "As far as you're concerned, I'm Mr. Campion himself—I'm operating under his express orders."

That's when I know for certain that Mr. Simpson is

operating under no one's orders but his own. The doctor falters for a moment, and then looks at me. He hardens on seeing my hopeful eyes. "Maybe so, but I must insist you go nowhere without talking to Mr. Temperley. He will answer to your employer if there are objections to how we handle the patient's release." As he exits, he calls back to Mr. Cosley, "Please stand outside the door, and do not let them leave until Mr. Temperley has returned." Cosley follows him out and shuts the door. A lock scrapes in the keyhole.

Mr. Simpson turns to me, his cool mask fallen and his eyes warm with concern. "Katherine, please tell me you're all right," he says in a whisper.

I nod, worried a sob will escape me. "I'm fine now, now that you're here. Henry did this to me. I can't even tell you all that I know of him now."

He doesn't pull away from me, from my hot whisper, though I know I must stink from my confinement. "Little of what you can tell me is news," he says into my ear. "For a while now I have suspected your cousin was not what he appeared to be. I had it on good authority, in fact, though it took me far too long to believe it. But we can't dwell on that now—first we must escape this place."

"The document you showed them, ordering my release?"

"A bluff. A convincing one, I thought, but no, I have no authority here. Which Mr. Temperley will be very aware of, once he returns. Now, quickly—any ideas on how we can get out?"

CHAPTER 27

I LOOK TOWARD THE door of the anteroom, imagining the guard on the other side in the corridor. "There's a window in Mr. Temperley's office," I whisper, nodding at the other door. "But even if we could get out that way, we'd still have to climb the gates."

"Then we'll climb the gates." Even in the dim room, his skin retains its warm glow, and he looks taller than I remember, pacing toward the office door. He tries the handle. "Locked." He looks back at me, concern in his eyes. "I have a horse waiting just beyond the grounds. Do you feel strong enough to run?"

"But there's nowhere *to* run," I say, starting to panic.

He takes two long steps back, and then rushes at the door, driving his foot into the wood. With a splintery shudder, it starts to give. He kicks it again, again, until it's hanging loosely on its hinges.

My mouth hangs open a bit as I stare. He smiles. "After you, Lady Katherine."

I get hold of myself and run to the office window, hearing the warning *slap* of approaching feet from the hallway beyond. Thankfully, Mr. Temperley felt no need to put bars on his own personal window.

"Quickly," William cries in a tight, authoritative voice. He props the door back into place, and then shoulders Mr. Temperley's desk against it, forming a barricade we both know can't last long.

At a glance I can see that the lock on the window is hopeless, so I grab blindly for the heavy brass paperweight on Temperley's desk. Shielding my face, I send it sailing through the window. Heavy fists beat against the blocked office door in response to the sound of shattering glass.

"Move aside, Katherine, now! They'll try to catch us on the grounds; we must hurry." William pushes his weight against the wooden framework of the window, shards of glass raining onto the thick tweed at his shoulders. Finally, the whole frame gives way. He leaps with surprising nimbleness to the ground below, and reaches back to retrieve me.

My leg scrapes across the window's raw edge as I tumble into his arms, but I barely wince. For one moment we're in each other's arms, surrounded by fallen stars of window glass. Then we run. Muck sucks at my feet, and each breath claws at my bruised ribs. I can see William checking his speed to keep apace with me, and I force myself to go faster, faster.

"Stop!" cries a voice at our backs. Cosley. "You cannot take that girl!"

The run to the gates is even more surreal by daylight. Once we reach them, William boosts me up, and we both begin to climb. The spikes at the top stab menacingly into the sky, but I can just slide my body between them. William stands fully upright atop the fence, slipping his legs through, then half climbs, half jumps to the ground below. He puts his arms up to meet mine, and then we've done it: We're over the gates.

His horse is loosely tied a few paces away. Though she's just a middle-aged brown mare, a bit temperamental if I had to guess, I think she is the most beautiful horse I've ever seen. Cosley and another guard, Mr. Smith, are pounding toward us as William fumbles her free. By the time she's untied, I've already swung myself into the saddle. "Let me take the reins," I cry. "Get up!"

He swings fluidly into place behind me as the men fumble at the locked gate. I hear Cosley scream a curse as we start to ride away. The horse pulls against me at first—cantankerous, just as I suspected. "Left, left!" cries William, his body warm and close behind. I swing the horse's head around, and soon I've got her in a hard trot, which I bring up into a gallop as soon as I've got a feel for the marshy road. The trees here are ancient and high; we ride between walls of black trunks. The shouts of Temperley's men quickly fade, replaced by the whipping cold air of the outside world.

When we're far enough away, William makes me slow down so that he can transfer his coat onto my shivering shoulders. "We must go back for Dorothy," I say through gritted teeth, wringing my frigid hands.

He reaches around my shoulders and takes my fingers in his, rubbing them to warmness. "You will never go back to that place," he says. "We'll help her as soon as we can, but you will never see the inside of Temperley's again."

The true desperation of my plight before his arrival starts to sink in, and my face streams with silent tears. We ride over sunken lanes and open fields, pausing to let the horse drink at streams as we pass them. My body is warmed by the coat and by his nearness. He directs me to the most remote paths, and we see no one. The world feels abandoned, as if we are the only riders for miles.

When it's become clear that we're not being followed, I break the silence. "How did you know where to find me?" I ask him. "I thought Henry would have told you I'd returned to America."

He's so close behind me that I can feel his voice in his chest. "That's what I was told, yes, when I came to the estate with the papers you requested. For five days running I'd been turned away at the door, told that you were indisposed or unable to see me. Finally, Mr. Carrick, that abominable man, told me you had set sail the day before. I didn't believe it, that you'd leave without saying good-bye, and I insisted on speaking to Henry. When Mr. Carrick went to fetch him, your dressing maid, Elsie, came to me. She looked frightened—so frightened I had to take her seriously when she told me you'd been spirited off in the night. When Henry did finally come to the door, he was as cool as ever, and repeated what Mr. Carrick had said.

"I rushed to Bristol, hoping that, of the two tales, Henry's was the true one. There I learned that you had not yet boarded a ship. So I thought on Elsie's claim, and surmised that you would be in this place. I have known of it for some years, because of payments made from Walthingham to the proprietors."

His tale first made me angry, and then warm with confused happiness.

"There is something else," he said. "As I waited at the harborside, I took out the watch you gave me. I thought I might figure out why it had stopped running, and began fiddling with it. But when I opened up the back . . . well, I discovered something remarkable."

"What?" I ask breathlessly.

"I'll show you soon. Let's keep on toward Walthingham. No, we're not going to the estate—but to somewhere safe, nearby."

We ride on. Mr. Simpson calls out from time to time to direct my path, but is otherwise silent. Always his hands are sturdy at my waist, keeping me upright and brave. Soon I start to recognize the terrain, and understand that we're nearing my land—the land that is mine to sell or to keep, that I will not allow to be stolen from me. "We mustn't get too close, Mr. Simpson. What if Henry is out riding today?"

"I'm taking you somewhere we won't be found. Here, let me have the reins."

He leads us straight through the trees and over the unused tracks. When we skirt the edge of Henry's quarry, I can orient myself again—the house is nearly a mile away as the crow flies, and we're moving away from it.

Now the sun has dipped to the level of our eyes. Orange light spills over the rocks and paints my skin gold. "We're here," he says softly, pulling the horse to a halt. He ties her up in a copse of trees, where she's unlikely to be seen, then turns to study the tree line.

"It should be just through there. Keep behind me, now."

The air, though biting cold, feels wonderfully fresh on my skin. We duck into a tunnel of tight-packed pines, the air between them heady with resin. I keep my eyes trained on Mr. Simpson's back under his dark tweed coat as he sweeps the trees' piney arms from our path. They shush closed behind us, hiding our trail from prying eyes. Soon the scent of pine and snow melt is overtaken by a more civilized smell—that of fire and cooking meat. I clutch the back of Mr. Simpson's coat.

"Almost there, Lady Katherine."

Finally, we break into a clearing just large enough for a single horse to graze. Across the way is a rock wall, with a low entrance carved into its front and darkness yawning beyond.

I think of my tiny cell at Temperley's, and the dingy, claustrophobic white of the straitjacket. My forehead feels suddenly damp. "I can't go in there."

"Hold tight to my hand." He extends it toward me, and I grasp at it and squeeze.

The smell of smoke is stronger here, and when we bend forward at the cavern entrance I can see that the darkness within is dancing, and laced with color. Once we've advanced a few yards, the rock ceiling is high enough for us to stand straight. A few paces more, and the pathway weaves left, leading to a cavern the size of a bedchamber at Walthingham. Near the back is a low, smoky fire, a spitted rabbit slung over it. The shapes of a table, a sofa, a mattress piled with furs swim out of the dim, and I nearly stumble over a slatted wooden chair piled with books.

Someone squats next to the fire, his head downturned. As we approach, the figure unfolds into a tall man with striking light eyes. I gasp and step behind William. McAllister watches us but does not speak, running rabbit-greasy hands over rough breeches.

"It's all right, Katherine," Mr. Simpson says. "He's going to help us."

"How do you know we can trust him?"

"I would trust him with anything. You see, Simpson is my mother's name. But Mr. McAllister is my father."

CHAPTER 28

I LOOK AT THE tall, tousle-haired lawyer, standing straight in his worn black tweed, then at the man behind the fire. His hair's a gray thatch and his clothes are shabby, and he looks at me even now with a curdled mixture of menace and sharp pride. But I can see a resemblance now, in the dignified way they hold themselves, in the bones of their faces. I breathe in, but I can't think of what to say.

McAllister surprises me by speaking first. His voice is different with his son in attendance. It softens and relaxes, and the faint burr of an Irish upbringing warms it. "I was no great family man," he says, "but it still came as a surprise to me when Mrs. McAllister left. Mrs. Simpson, she called herself after that—her family name. Passed herself off as a widow, I believe. Isn't that right, boy?"

Mr. Simpson nods silent assent.

"It seems a strange thing to me, a terrible thing, to wish for a man's death like that." He holds up a hand, as if to quell his son's protests. "But I see now, and saw it even then, that she had to do it. I was no great family man, as I said, and she did what she had to. William was small when she took him, and I followed after her. I tracked her right to the very boardinghouse where they were hiding. I had the sense not to talk to her right away—they wouldn't have let her stay, if I'd come running in. But I caught her on her way to church next morning, with little William wrapped up warm in her arms. She was always a good ma.

"I wished I could remind her of our courting days, but truth is we didn't really have them. Or I could make promises of being a better man for her, but I didn't want to tell lies. Sentimentality's never suited me. So I only asked her if she'd come home with me. I told her we never need talk of it again, and that William would be too small ever to remember. And she pressed my hand and shook her head, and did not say another word to me again. Not ever. And that was the last I saw of my son until he was a man grown, a solicitor working for Crowne & Crowne. You can never say I wasn't proud, or grateful to Lord Walthingham for all he did for him."

"But what did he do?" I ask, watching the man's sad face through the trailing smoke of his campfire.

"He was my benefactor," says William, watching my face. "He took pity on my mother and paid for my boarding school. Then my legal training at the Inns. He also put in a word for me with Crowne & Crowne—they were already his solicitors."

McAllister breaks in. "My son looks ashamed now—we McAllisters were never much for giving credit where credit's due, or for admitting that we had help along the way. Lucky for you, young lady, the boy's got much of his mother in him, too."

William does look flushed, but continues. "I lost my mother to illness two years ago. When she was dying she told me the truth: that my father was alive and working for Walthingham. At the time I knew your grandfather only as the man of the house. It was only in her final days that my mother revealed his part in my advancement, something he had not wished her to do. I came to the house to thank him, and to meet my father." His eyes meet McAllister's, briefly.

"We quickly realized that too much time had passed for ours to be more than a passing acquaintance," he says, low. I can see that this pains him—shames him, even.

"It's all right, William," his father offers. "I'd rather have a son who faces things honestly than one who flatters with his words. Like that blasted Henry Campion."

The change that comes over his features when he speaks Henry's name is extreme. I see again the hardened, criminal presence that I once imagined stalking the woods of Walthingham.

"My boy came back looking for a father," continues McAllister. "And he very nearly found one. Not me, though. Lord Walthingham."

"That's not true—" William protests, but his father cuts him off.

"Walthingham and my son were men of a similar mind. The master had driven his own son off, as you well know, lady, and that nephew of his was the very picture of his own father: a dissolute, a charmer, a snake with a handsome face, who had married Walthingham's only sister. Lord Walthingham could never bear the thought of leaving it all to him, though he knew he'd likely have to. But Campion got to thinking that William might be given an inheritance—some small piece that would lessen his own part of the store when your grandfather died. It seemed, though, like it would be many years before that happened. Your grandfather was the halest man that I knew— and the best rider." McAllister glared and he folded his arms. "Not the sort to fall and snap his neck."

His meaning becomes clear to me. "You think there was foul play?"

The firelight finds the old man's eyes, and they glow with hooded intelligence. "Henry Campion was broken after the war. Your grandfather saw it and did his best to make a son of him. They rode out together every day. I saw them setting out together one morning, early, though no groom accompanied them. Just before midday, Campion came back saying his horse had thrown a shoe. When Lord Walthingham still hadn't come back for luncheon, they went looking. Found him deep in the forest with his head stoved in."

I feel sick. "Grace never told me about a head injury. She said he died from a broken neck, instantly."

McAllister sniffed angrily. "His neck was snapped, that's right enough, but he hung on for two days, unable to move an inch. Never have I seen a man so pale as your cousin. But he did not grieve—he feared. Feared, I think, that your grandfather would wake, and tell the truth."

"The truth," I breathe. "Sir, do you think that my cousin— did you ever tell the magistrate of your suspicions?"

"I am not a man to make accusations lightly, but nor do I

hold my peace when I have a suspicion that something's not right. Campion was at the bedside constantly in those two days that your grandfather hung on to his life. But on the second morning, he stepped out long enough to see me—and to tell me that I was to leave Walthingham at once. I know why he did it. You see, I'm the only one who knows the grounds the way he does. I'm the only one who might have seen something—might have seen whatever it was that happened the day your grandfather died. I made no fuss, but set straight out to find William in London. 'His Lordship's son might still be alive,' I told him. 'In America. If not, he may have heirs of his own, who would be first in line for the estate.' Anything to keep it out of Campion's bloody hands. That's right: My son was the one who tracked you down. Not that he believed me about Campion until now. He inherited his mother's expectations of goodness."

He leans forward on his knees, as if this much talk has tired him out. Then he tilts his head up to eye me balefully. "And if I steal an animal from your land from time to time just to keep myself alive, after all my service to your family, I don't see as you should fault it!"

William shuffles his feet, embarrassed by this final outburst, but my mind is blooming with all I've been told. "Tell me now, please. What did you find in the watch?"

The watch gleams in the firelight when he pulls it from his pocket. "Here, look. You can see why it no longer worked." With careful fingers, he opens its back and turns it to show me: an empty cavity where the mechanism should be, and inside it a crumpled scrap of white. "Someone removed the gears and put this in their place."

I can tell by the way he dips his head as he hands the note to me that he's already read it. And who wouldn't read a message secreted into the back of a broken watch? The words on the page are blotted and misshapen, but their meaning is true:

To Ladie Kathrin:

I do belief that "he watches over us all," yore George, my mother and father, and the Lord Walthingham alike. Yore trust is mistook—I am the one who helped Henry Campion do his teribul deed. He slew George in the wud, and I cam upon him. He gayve me munnie wich could not be eenuf for the sale of my everlasting sole, yet I tuk it to hid the bodie of yore brother. I am sorry beyond messure for wat I did, and feer my lief will not be long. I miss-trust Campion. If you fined this letter it is becus I am done for, and at his hand. Do not trust him. Think of me a litle, and speek a prayr. Do not comend my sole to GOD, becus it is him not you wat will deside my fayt heerafter.

John Hayes

To see proof of my suspicions at last, in black-and-white, is too much for me to bear. "My brother," I cry. "My trusting brother! He was Henry's cousin; we share blood! Murdering his own family, to feed his own greed—how can it be possible?" The close heat of the cavern combines with my renewed horror, and I feel myself start to swoon. No sooner do my knees dip than William's arms are around me, and he leads me to a chair.

"This is a shock, Katherine." William cups my chin in his

hands, forcing me to look at him. "And I pray that you do not lose yourself under the weight of it. But despite what you've read, I still counsel caution. This is not proof—he will say we've forged it. He has a very old family name at his back, and allies like Dr. Ebner. Even Mr. Dowling seems to have been taken in by your cousin. Henry Campion is cunning and has gotten away with his misdeeds thus far. But"—he holds up a finger—"I think that lately he has gotten careless."

"We'll catch him unaware," I say. "And if the law can't make him pay for my brother's death, I will do it myself."

"Don't be reckless, Katherine," William says softly. "I promise you, your brother's death will not go unpunished."

I summon the hardness of heart that protected me through the past five nights in a windowless cell. "I'll get him to talk. But before I do, we'll need the magistrate."

CHAPTER 29

THE SUN IS just cresting the hills that cup my lands when we first spy Walthingham in the distance. We ride toward it in a rented carriage—I don't want Henry to recognize the Dowlings' coach and driver. Jane is beside me, pressing my hand. Her usual good humor has been replaced by a worn sadness, and she seems unable to stop apologizing to me. Her betrayal is so very small, in the face of things, that it's all I can do to assure her again and again that she is forgiven.

It's half past seven in the morning. For the first time since the funeral, I'm dressed in neither black nor gray, but in a blue dress belonging to Jane—too pale for me, but less tight around the hips than it would have been before my stay in Temperley's. Though Jane's two maids nearly drowned me in honey-scented water last night, I can still feel the grime of that place on my skin.

"Are you certain," Jane says hoarsely, "that you don't want me to come with you? Perhaps if I speak to him, he will be more likely to confess."

Even after all that she's learned about Henry, I can see that she still cares for him, still dreams that he might be worthy of her affections. It's hard to kill love so quickly.

"There's no need," I say.

"But what if Elsie doesn't play along?" says Jane. "You could be in danger. If my father and William—"

"She will," I say. *I hope she will.*

I feel George's presence strongly today, his breath at my shoulder. He would forgive her without question, as many times as she asked. He loved recklessly, lived recklessly, and was cut down by a cowardly and broken man. I send a prayer upward and kiss Jane's cheek. "My plan depends on my going alone. I won't leave that place without his confession."

For a quarter of an hour, I watch the great husk of Walthingham grow larger in my sight. When we finally reach the drive, Jane is nearly shaking, clutching at my hand. Her fear makes me feel less afraid. I offer her a small smile, then adjust my hat to further obscure my features.

Mr. Carrick answers my knock. The expression on his face does not make up for my ordeal, but it helps. "Lady . . . Randolph!" he sputters. "How did you . . ."

"Take my things, Carrick. Good God, have you never been taught manners?" I drop my hat and cloak into his arms and walk toward the front parlor. "Send Henry down to meet me at once."

I can hear Carrick clattering up the stairs, forgetting to move with his usual air of stately arrogance. I survey the placid room: A fire is low in the hearth, and thick, fanciful tap-estries line the walls. In one a unicorn lies in a clearing, tended by a maiden whose hair is woven through with golden threads. Just beyond the clearing is a stitched black beast, watching the girl through the trees. But as I look at the unicorn's horn, hovering close to her heart, I wonder: Is the beast menacing her, or moving to save her from the unicorn? I will never again be fooled by mere appearances.

I'm about to check behind the huge curtains on the far-thest wall when I hear a footstep at the door. It's Elsie and she gives me a warm, quick smile before turning and darting away. I know then that she has done her part. Now it is up to me.

"So, you've returned to Walthingham."

Henry strides into the room, speaking without preamble or pleasantry. His face is dark above the frothing white of his open collar. He looks me over once, dismissively, before mov-ing to make himself a drink. But he cannot fool me—his hands shake as they play over the crystal decanters. It's not until he's had one belt of whiskey, and then another, that he speaks again. His tone is conversational, light. "Have you com-pleted your treatment, cousin? Or have you managed what would be a quite impressive escape?"

"You were warned about me, Henry—I'm a wildcat. Though I have had help in getting here."

He laughs, quite naturally. "From the lawyer, I suppose. It took me longer than it should have to put two and two together. He's the son of that trash, McAllister, isn't he? Both of them will pay for their deeds against me before this day is out."

His false serenity is beginning to slip, revealing the

ugliness below. I seize the opportunity to push him over the edge. "I know what you've done, Henry. And I have proof."

He begins to walk in my direction, as if to box me against the wall. I step to my right, toward the curtain, keeping the open door in my sight. "And what proof might that be, Katherine? The certificate of insanity? Perfectly sound, and for your own protection. You were mad with grief over your brother's death."

"Give it up, Henry. I have a letter from John. A *real* letter, not a despicable forgery. It was hidden in the watch that *you* must have given to him. A cheap piece of 'evidence,' and I've caught you out with it in the end. But I will offer you more kindness than you offered me: Admit what you've done, and I will let you leave my house immediately. You may take nothing, say no good-byes. Just admit what you did to George, and you may leave by that door."

"Oh, may I?" He laughs, a wild and desperate sound. "May I leave the only home I've ever known, which stands on a hillside I fought the French to protect? May I leave it now, to an unschooled American orphan who would sell it to the highest bidder? May I make the great name of Walthingham into a pile of dust, and myself into a crippled joke? You give me leave to do this, Katherine?" His voice is rising to a shriek. I will myself not to shrink away.

"You're a coward, Henry Campion. My family name is not yours. You dishonor yourself and your people and this land. How did you do it? Did you kill my brother with a rock, the way you did my grandfather?"

"Ah, you've been speaking to McAllister, have you? Your grandfather's was a mercy killing. He'd gone soft: He was as bad as you. He was likely to have left the estate to that country-born mutt, that lawyer! Nobody who remembers Lord Walthingham now can say a bad word against him, because I killed him before he could destroy his own legacy."

My heart thumps. He's said the magic words—he's admitted to murder. I should stop now, but I can't. "And what of my brother?" I say softly. "Was it the same way with him?"

"Your brother was worthless. An artist and a dreamer, who could barely keep his eyes from the window long enough to learn what was required of him. He thought that learning a few dance steps was enough to call himself Lord Walthingham. He didn't deserve this place."

"He didn't deserve to *die!*" I shout.

"Perhaps not," says Henry, "but what else could I do? No one but I can protect Walthingham."

He shifts toward me, suddenly crafty. "Where is John's letter now? You've got it in your pocket there? Hand it over, and I'll go quietly. I'll go to London straightaway. I never meant you harm, Katherine."

I need no more proof of his insanity than his belief that I might be taken in by this transparent lie. "The letter is with Jane Dowling, on its way to the magistrate. By the afternoon, you will be taken in to account for your crimes."

He turns his back toward me, facing the fading fire. "So I have a few hours yet." In one fluid motion, he lunges forward and snatches a poker from beside the hearth. "And what's to stop me from killing you now? Why should I not bash your head in, and burn your body before the sun's reached its height?"

As he advances toward me, I shrink against the curtain,

really afraid at last, but it moves behind me, and two men step out from its shelter, into the light.

"Because we will stop you, Henry Campion," says William, his color up and his eyes hard. Mr. Dowling stands beside him, holding a shotgun in two hands and huffing as though he's been running. He looks at the man who might have been his son-in-law through eyes hooded with sadness and fatigue. Just as we planned, they came in through the rear of the house, courtesy of Elsie. "You'll come with me now, Henry," Mr. Dowling says. "To go on trial for the murders of Lord Walthingham and his heir, George Randolph."

In the initial shock of the men's entrance, Henry's eyes filled with fear, and his hand with its poker dropped to his side. But now I see his gaze go blank and white before he springs into motion: He flings the poker at William, striking his temple and sending him stumbling back into the wall. Henry reels from the room, heavy on his bad leg but moving with more speed than I'd thought him capable of. "Stop him, Carrick!" I scream uselessly—even now, the butler will have his loyalties. I realize Henry is making for the house's west wing and start to follow. Jane's shoes pinch and restrict me. I balance myself against a wall for one quick moment, wrenching them from my feet so I can run.

"No, Kat! Wait!" cries William.

The door to the wing hangs open, and Henry's limping form is speeding around a far corner. I run past the covered furniture, through the room that held my brother's body, then stop in place, spinning around in confusion. Then I see him, through the nearest window. Its glass is slightly warped, and his form looks off, twisted, rushing in the direction of the stables. I wrench the window open, and then, for the second time in as many days, I vault myself over the ledge. The frozen grass crunches below me as I pursue Henry—ignoring the biting pain in my feet, focusing only on the breaths filling my abused rib cage, and on closing the gap between us. But I'm too late. Even as I'm pounding toward the stables, he's emerging wild-eyed, leading a saddled horse. He vaults himself onto it and starts riding hard toward the woods.

The other animals are shifting restlessly in their stalls as I enter, driven to nervous distraction by Henry's wild behavior and mine. None are wearing saddles. I choose the great gray stallion that Henry rode the day of the hunt, and I'm on his back before he's even out of the stall. The animal is unused to being ridden bareback, but he's my cousin's favorite for a reason: Soon we're flying through the open air, toward the space in the trees where broken branches signal Henry's avenue of escape. I smile in grim satisfaction, thinking of the men that Mr. Dowling has stationed near the clearing around McAllister's old cottage. They will likely cut Henry off before I can reach him. But I long to see my cousin taken in, and ride on.

He's just within my sights when he reaches the clearing around the gamekeeper's cottage. I know he's spotted the men standing there with their dogs, because he veers to one side, pulling his horse's head hard to the left and breaking into the woodland.

"Stop!" I scream. "Give yourself up, Henry Campion!"

He knows the woods better than I do, but I'm a better rider. For a moment I lose him in the half-light among the trees, and then I spy him through a break in the branches.

"Faster, faster," I urge my mount, digging in with my knees and straining to stay behind my cousin. Just before he slips again from my sights, I realize he's been leading us in a great circle over the land, and is now headed back toward the quarry.

My body is low over the horse, my hands tangled in its mane and my legs starting to quiver, when I hear a long, terrible scream. The sound rakes my skin with chilly fingers, and for a moment I cannot tell whether it's come from Henry's horse or its rider. We're racing now along the weed-covered track that wends its way alongside the quarry. Following the sound of the cry, I bring the panting horse carefully through the trees leading to the quarry's edge.

There I find Henry's mount, riderless and stamping. Its sides are streaked with froth, but it looks to be unhurt. I whip my head wildly from side to side, searching for Henry, for the trampled bushes that might mark his path on foot. There's nothing to see, and finally I slip from my horse's back.

Carefully, I advance toward the agitated animal, looking over my shoulder to be sure that Henry is not at my back, waiting to push me onto the rocks below. From far away, I hear the sounds of Mr. Dowling's men, crashing through the woods on foot. Their dogs are baying. I pick my way barefoot over the gravelly ground at the quarry's edge, where the earth gives way to a sheer stone wall. I peek over it into the jagged valley, and gasp.

Henry is stretched across two boulders far below. His head lies lower than his chest, frozen at a queer, gut-wrenching angle. He's perfectly still. On instinct, I look up; already two crows circle above us, scenting fresh death on the air.

I grip my arms with cold fingers, crouching in bare feet

so numb and raw I can only dimly sense them. What made him fall? The horse is uninjured, and the approaching men are still too distant. As I lean forward, barely able to wrench my gaze from the broken body below, a near-subliminal sound raises the fine hairs on my neck. I turn slowly, my heart pumping with dread.

A little ways from me, a pile of boulders rises from the earth, stacked like a cairn. Atop it, black as nightmares and breathing in fast, hot spurts, is an impossibly large, yellow-eyed cat. Staring back at the thing, I forget to breathe, until my chest starts to ache and I tip forward in the grass. It glares at me, panting on my knees in the damp morning, then turns and pads silently away, disappearing with a leap into the dark space between two trunks.

Mr. Dowling's men finally break through the trees. They call out for Henry, their dogs straining toward the quarry. Mr. Simpson, his face flushed and smeared with dirt from the chase, rushes to my side, guiding me to my feet and into his arms. I hear the breath catch in his throat as he spots Henry's corpse below.

"It's over, Katherine," he murmurs. "It's over now." His heart pounds against my ear, and I think for a moment of telling him what I've seen. I squint at the place where the animal disappeared, and wonder if I imagined its presence. But the spooked horse, and the man lying on the rocks below, tell me it was real.

CHAPTER 30

G RACE'S CARRIAGE CRESTS the rise and is gone, my cousin just a faint outline inside it. Only the birds calling from the menagerie herald her leaving. I watch the carriage disappear, carrying her to the home of an elderly aunt, and then continue on my way into the woods. The air around me feels brighter, just knowing Grace won't be at the estate when I return.

There have been three days of comings and goings. Mr. Dowling did what he could to keep Henry's name out of the mud, but servants will talk. I didn't even watch them load Henry's coffin and take it away. Crowne & Crowne are handling his burial, somewhere far from Walthingham. Of course, the house is not the same without him, and without his sister. Few of the best families will look at the Randolphs in the same way after everything that's happened, but it doesn't bother me in the slightest. I can't imagine I'll be hosting many balls here.

I never had the chance to ask Grace why she deserted me the night Henry dragged me away to Temperley's, and she never came to me to offer any excuse. Whatever brittle relationship we had is shattered and irreparable with her brother's death. Even if I could bring myself to interrogate her, I doubt I could discover the truth. She might claim it was a sisterly concern—that she in fact believed me hysterical and in need of medical help—and I would not swear that she was lying. Or if she was, even she herself did not realize it. Grace lived a strange, sheltered life until the stark reality of the present. I see now that she's formed an existence based on the certainties of class and the rules of decorum, but without those supports, her delicate world is nothing but confection. I do not doubt she loved her brother, and the true horror of his deeds will have shaken her to her core. I hope she finds some peace, somewhere.

"You look troubled, Lady Walthingham. Do you regret Miss Campion's departure?" Mr. Simpson is wearing a light-weight coat and his customary serious expression, but I know now the gentleness and good humor that lie beneath that exterior. I can still see the raised scar over his left brow, where Henry struck him, but it's softening with the passing days.

"I can't say that I do," I reply, smiling. I've set our course toward the bridge. I may never like that spot in wintertime, but today the light is soft, and warm on our faces. "I'm only thinking of the women still left at Temperley's."

"Not Temperley's anymore," he reminds me softly. "Soon it will officially be the George Randolph Hospital and Children's

Home. Some of the former inmates have returned to their families, for better or worse. But many of them truly have no place to go."

"We'll keep them under the new staff," I say. "Anyone who wants to stay."

"I never have seen someone give way to a sale so quickly as Mr. Temperley," says William, smiling. "I'd like to think it was my legal skill that did it, but perhaps we should credit the influence of the magistrate."

Among Temperley's women with a home to go to is Dorothy. She's still weak from her imprisonment, but reuniting with Elsie makes her stronger every day.

"You are still trying to find Dorothy's baby, aren't you?" I ask quietly.

"We've reached only dead ends," he says with regret. "But she will have many opportunities to work with children at the hospital."

I smile at him and try to let that be enough. I'm certain, at least, that my brother would approve of the way I'm spending our family fortune. We have enough of it, after all—there was no need, in the end, for me to sell the estate.

"Soon we'll have few opportunities to meet like this." Mr. Simpson doesn't look at me as he speaks. "Your hospital will be open, and you will, I hope, have no further need for a lawyer."

"You hope?"

We walk to the middle of the bridge and pause. Our reflections in the water are backed by a sea of open sky. My hand still lies on his arm.

"I didn't mean—it's just that, I hope you can live a life with no need of legal help."

I speak impulsively, my heart in my throat. "I'm grateful for what you've done for me. But do you think I walk out with you daily because of the legal advice you can give?"

In the lapping water below, his expression is too blurred to read. I dare not turn to look at his face.

"And do you think," he says softly, "that I make the trip from Bath each day because I so love the countryside? But, Katherine . . ." He pauses a moment. "I should not even call you that. You are a lady, Lady Walthingham now. I'm not even a partner at Crowne & Crowne."

I can't help it: I slap my palm in frustration against the rail of the bridge. "If titles and riches were what determined the decency of a man, then I would be standing here in love with my cousin, Henry Campion, not you."

In the moment of dense, shimmering silence that follows, I'm struck by the import of what I've just said. Mr. Simpson turns to me and seizes my hand, his voice taut with excitement. "Say that again, Katherine."

I take a deep breath. "William Simpson, I don't care what you are, I care *who* you are. And I love you."

I dare look into his eyes at last. And as he leans his face toward mine, I think with joy of just how little Grace would approve of my kissing the family lawyer. But I am the sole remaining Randolph of Walthingham Hall, and I think I will keep my business my own.

I turn my face upward to meet his.